Jammy Dodgers in Deadly Danger

Praise for the Jammy Dodgers series:

'The Jammy Dodgers are wickedly stupendous'
Harry, aged 11

'Scary and funny — it was great!' Oliver, aged 8

'Extremely exciting and intriguing . . . made me feel
like I was really there. I can't wait for the next one'
Ben, aged 11

'The books I like are usually funny or exciting, but
the Jammy Dodgers books are funny *and* exciting'
Sasha, aged 8

'Read this plaguy quick' Tabitha, aged 12

Jammy Dodgers in Deadly Danger

BOWERING SIVERS

MACMILLAN CHILDREN'S BOOKS

First published 2007 by Macmillan Children's Books
a division of Macmillan Publishers Limited
20 New Wharf Road, London N1 9RR
Basingstoke and Oxford
www.panmacmillan.com

Associated companies throughout the world

ISBN: 978-0-230-01552-4

1 3 5 7 9 8 6 4 2

A CIP catalogue record for this book is available from
the British Library.

Typeset by Intype Libra Ltd
Printed and bound in Great Britain by Mackays of Chatham plc, Kent

For John, Jane and Peter,
the Bowering half of my name, with love

In memory of Helen Lawrie,
kindest and most generous of friends.
And Sable and Hannah, who gave us such joy

Acknowledgements

For my editor, Sarah Dudman, who takes what I write and makes it better, and for Talya Baker, my desk editor, a 'nitpicker' (her word, not mine) par excellence.

Thanks also to the staff of the Museum of London, the Museum in Docklands, the Metropolitan Police Historical Collection, the Thames Police Museum and the City of Westminster Archives Centre.

Contents

I

1

All Londoners went to the Easter fair at Greenwich, a small town on the Thames a few miles east of London. Well before dawn the roads were already full of hackney coaches, cabs, omnibuses, carts, gigs, sociables and chaises crammed to bursting with men, women and children chattering and laughing and swilling ale and ginger beer by the barrelful.

The Perkinskis travelled in a wagon that Uncle Arthur had hired from a pig farmer in a remote village called Wembley. Although the wagon was big, it was still a tight squeeze for Gran, Ma and Pa, their daughter, Kate, their three sons, Jem, Ned and Billy, and a vast assortment of aunts, uncles, nephews, nieces and cousins. And so as it lumbered along, lurching into potholes and sinking up to its wheel hubs in muddy ruts, there was a great deal of jostling and shoving among the family and ill-tempered cries of 'Do get your pesky elbow out of my ribs, Jack!' and 'That's twice you've poked me in the eye, Em!'

And the smell didn't sweeten their humour either. Unfortunately the pig farmer had been rather casual about cleaning up the wagon and there was a plentiful reminder of his animals on the floor and sides. As Uncle Percy remarked, 'Pigs're never fussy about where they do it.' And they seemed to have done it everywhere.

A donkey cart drew level with them, and its occupants, catching sight of Pa Perkinski, shouted, 'It's the Beast! It's the Beast!' 'Who're you're fighting today?' they asked, for Pa was a prize fighter and there were contests at the fair every year. 'Is it Killer Kelly?'

'Nah.' Pa shook his head. 'I flattened him last time. 'Sides he's in clink now for pastin' two crushers. I'm goin' to fight Ahmed the Assassin.'

Ahmed was famous, not so much for his skill in the ring as for his good looks. Pa, on the other hand, had the kind of face even a mother would be hard pressed to love. His nose had been flattened so often it spread from one ear to the other and his mouth was filled with gums and not much else, which is why the contest between him and Ahmed had been dubbed 'Beauty and the Beast'.

But it was Pa who was the favourite, and Jem, Ned and Billy swelled with pride as the crowd began to cheer their father, calling out, 'Good luck, Beast!'

'I got good money on you,' cried one man. 'A whole crown. You'd better not lose or my old woman'll kill me.'

'He never loses,' cried another. 'Three cheers for the Beast! Hip! Hip! . . .'

Pa doffed his hat, revealing a head as hairless as a golf ball, and beamed toothlessly as the crowd bellowed, 'Hurrah!'

The Perkinskis made slow progress because Ma and Cousin Annie insisted on stopping the wagon every so often to pick daffodils and tulips from the gardens they passed, and so by the time they arrived at the fair it was well under way.

A horrendous din greeted them – people firing pistols and clanging gongs, tradesmen shouting their wares, clowns ringing bells and banging drums, wild animals in their cages roaring and, above it all, the strident noise of at least six brass bands in fierce contest with one another.

Little Billy jumped up and down clapping his hands excitedly, but the rest of his family looked glum, for a troupe of midget magicians and conjurers had taken their favourite campsite and refused to budge.

'We gypsies've been doin' business on this very spot for fifty years or more,' grumbled Gran, who had brought a sackful of her fake cosmetics, quack medicines and magic potions to sell to the rich and gullible.

'Gypsies? You're never no gypsies,' snarled one of the midgets. 'That's a load of hocus-pocus.'

'You're right, Shandy,' shouted the others. 'They're just jumped-up tinkers giving themselves airs.'

Now if there was anything guaranteed to put Pa in a rage it was someone telling him he wasn't a gypsy.

'I'll have you know we come from a long line of gypsies,' he said indignantly, elbowing his way though the crowd that had gathered to watch. 'Matter of fact, we're from Egypt, where all true gypsies come from.'

'Nah, we aren't, Pa,' piped up Billy. 'We come from Devil's Acre.'

'I meant hundreds of years ago, you ninny,' snapped Pa, glaring at him.

'Devil's Acre? Huh! Just what I thought. They're a load of riff-raff from the most poisonous rookery

4

in London,' sneered Shandy, who was the midgets' leader. 'Well, we're not movin' off this site, specially for a chicken from Devil's Acre.' And reaching forward, he pulled an egg from between Pa's knees.

The crowd guffawed and clapped approval.

'Who're you callin' a chicken?' demanded Pa, incensed.

'You,' retorted Shandy.

'Look me straight in the eye and say that again if you dare,' thundered Pa. And he drew himself up to his full height of well over six feet and swelled out his chest until it looked like a large barrel of ale.

Shandy also drew himself up to his full height, looked Pa straight in the belly button and, flapping his arms as if they were wings, crowed, 'Cock-a-doodle-do!'

'Don't get rumbumptious with me, my lad,' Pa warned him. 'You're askin' for a pastin' and you're goin' to get it if you're not careful. I'm not called the Beast for nothin', you know.'

'Course not,' chuckled Shandy. 'Anyone can see you're a stupid great ox.'

'Right, I've had enough lip from you. I'm tellin' you for the last time – get off our patch.'

'No, we won't,' shouted the midgets, with one voice.

'All right, I'll fight the lot of you single-handed.'

'Well said, Beast,' cried his fans, as Pa took off his velveteen jacket and handed it to Uncle Arthur, who was his manager and trainer when he wasn't selling wilted vegetables from a cart in Covent Garden. 'You're a real sport.'

'I'll fight you alone,' said Shandy. 'I don't need no help from the others.'

'Lor', he's plucky for such a littl'un,' said someone in the crowd.

'Plucky? Paff! More like queer in the attic, if you ask me,' sniggered Uncle Arthur, tapping the side of his head. 'The Beast'll make mincemeat of him.'

'This fight's got to be all fair and above board so we'll need a referee. Could I have a volunteer, please?' said Pa. 'Course, it's got to be someone who doesn't know me or my opponent.'

A man stepped out of the crowd but before he could say anything Pa grabbed his brother George and dragging him forward he said, 'Thank you, sir. That's good of you to agree.'

'Give me some of them coloured streamers,' said Jem, turning to his mother, who had a tray of knick-knacks suspended from her neck.

'What for?'

'I'll show you.' And taking some of the brightly

coloured papers his mother sold on the streets of London, Jem tore them into small pieces and waved them above his head shouting, 'Get your tickets for the big fight, ladies'n gen'lemen! A penny for the front row, ha'penny for the back. Get your tickets for the big fight between Bert the Beast and Shandy the Shrimp.'

'We don't have to pay,' said someone indignantly.

'Course not,' agreed Jem. 'But if you don't there won't be no fight.'

Reluctantly people thrust their hands in their pockets and brought out the required coins which they exchanged for a 'ticket' from a grinning Jem.

'Everyone's paid up,' he said to his father. 'You can start the fight.'

'I don't suppose it'll go more'n a hundred rounds,' said Pa, while the crowd fell about laughing. 'This here,' he pointed at Shandy, 'this here's the fiercest man I ever met. I'm so frightened I can't hardly stop myself tremblin'. I'm all of a jelly like,' he guffawed, raising his arms above his head and shaking them so that everyone could see his bulging biceps.

'Ladies'n gen'lemen, the fight will now begin,' shouted Uncle George, raising his hand for silence. 'London Prize Ring Rules apply and the winner takes this pitch. So to speed things up, seein' as how the Beast's obviously goin' to win, would you lot –' he waved at the troupe of midgets – 'move your stuff right now so's we can take over straight afterwards.'

'Stow it!' cried one of them angrily.

'Yeh, take a carrot,' shouted another. 'We're not movin' from this pitch . . . Never!'

'NEVER!' shouted the others.

'Right, Bert . . . I mean Beast, flatten him!' said Uncle George, pointing at Shandy.

'Give him one in the bread basket!' yelled a man, miming a punch at the midget's stomach.

'Darken his daylights!' hollered another, urging Pa to give Shandy a couple of black eyes.

Pa raised his fists and squared up to Shandy, who put his hands on his hips and stared at him scornfully.

'Well, come on then, tiddler,' said Pa. 'Put up a bunch of fives and start fightin'.'

'Nah,' said Shandy, refusing to raise his fists, 'you start.'

'Why should I start?'

'Why should I?'

The crowd was beginning to grow restive.

'Look here, I didn't pay good brass to hear a

couple of parrots squawkin' at each other,' complained a man in the front row. 'If you clack boxes don't start fightin' plaguy quick I want my money back.'

At that, Jem turned deathly pale. 'Go on Pa, Lor's sake,' he hissed at his father. 'Wipe him out!'

Gathering all his strength, Pa took a mighty swipe at the midget. It was the kind of blow that would normally have felled a bull elephant but Shandy ducked at the last moment so that Pa missed and swung himself round and round like a spinning top.

Seizing his opportunity, while Pa staggered dizzily from one side of the makeshift ring to the other, Shandy charged into the back of his knees. The big man buckled and fell on his face with a grunt, at which point Shandy grabbed his head, thrust it between his legs and sat on it.

'Get up, Beast!' shouted the crowd.

'Yeh, Pa, get up!' yelled Jem, Ned and Billy.

But Pa couldn't do anything other than flail his arms and legs like a beached octopus. Not only could he not get up, he couldn't breathe. Nor could he tell anyone about his dangerous shortage of breath because Shandy was pressing his face into the mud.

'Start countin', ref,' urged the troupe of midgets. 'Count to ten.'

'Well, I don't know . . .' Uncle George stroked his chin thoughtfully while Shandy bounced up and down on Pa's head as if it was a rubber ball. 'It wasn't fair play. Your man cheated like a brick.'

'He didn't! He didn't! He got the Beast down fair'n square. Start countin'!'

'Oh, all right. One . . . two . . . three . . .' Uncle George counted very slowly, giving his brother time to throw off Shandy and get back on his feet. But Pa had gone strangely quiet. In fact he was so quiet he could have been mistaken for someone who was half dead, which he was.

'Four . . . Five . . .'

Most of Pa's fans seemed to have dropped away, for the crowd began to stamp and jeer.

'Six . . . Seven . . .'

'Go on! Go on!' the crowd urged.

'Seven . . . er . . . I forget what comes next,' said Uncle George, giving his brother an encouraging kick in the ribs to revive him.

'Eight, you stupe! Eight!'

'Oh yeh, that's right. I never was no good at numbers. I remember when I was a little kid learnin' to count and my mum said, "George," she said, cos that was my name at that time – well, matter of fact it still is – she said, "George," she said, "you are such a—"'

'GET ON WITH IT!' screamed the crowd, near to hysteria by now.

'Oh, all right,' muttered Uncle George, looking sadly at his brother, who was still lying on the ground with Shandy bouncing on his head, 'eight, nine, ten.'

Immediately Shandy sprang up and strutted up and down to a round of enthusiastic applause and cries of, 'Well done, littl'un. It's brains that count, not brawn.'

After a minute or two Pa sat up very slowly, his face caked in mud. 'I could've . . . I could've thrown him off,' he gasped, 'but I didn't want to hurt him. So in the interests of fair play,' he said, his voice sounding like a death rattle, 'I'm prepared to call it a draw and let them lot have our site. But next year,' he added, dragging himself upright with the help of Uncle George and Uncle Arthur, 'I won't be so soft-hearted. I'm warnin' them now, if they try to steal it again I'll give them a right jacketin'.'

A few cheers but many more jeers greeted this but above them all Jem's voice could be heard shouting, 'Get your tickets now for next year's return match, ladies'n gen'lemen. Twopence for the front row, a penny for the back.'

2

All the best places close to the fair had been taken by mid-morning so the Perkinskis were forced to pitch their camp half a mile away. They grumbled and groaned about what an awful site it was, not at all what they were used to, as if their normal habitat was a picturesque square in Mayfair or Belgravia instead of a squalid slum with dark, dingy alleyways and tumbledown houses. But nothing could spoil the excitement Jem, Ned and Billy felt. For a few precious days they were away from the cobblestone streets clogged with traffic, away from Devil's Acre, the stinking yard in Westminster piled high with rubbish and manure they called home, away from the dilapidated caravan they shared with their parents. For a few, precious days they saw trees and bushes and flowers instead of crumbling walls and broken windows and overflowing cesspits. And best of all they could sleep on the soft, springy grass instead of on rough straw mattresses teeming with fleas, lice and bugs.

While Uncle Arthur unhitched the horses from the wagon Ma got out the big iron pot she used for boiling everything, from gruel to Pa's trousers, and sent Jem to fetch water and Ned and Billy to look for sticks to make a fire. When the water had boiled Ma made everyone tea, which they took turns to drink out of two dirty, chipped cups.

'What about breakfast, Ma?' said Billy.

'You had breakfast.'

'But that was hours ago, Ma, and I only had a bit of bread. It was so small I couldn't hardly see it.'

'Well, if you do well at the fair today you'll get a bigger bit tonight.'

Billy heaved a deep sigh. He longed to have fun at the fair, to wander past the stalls piled high with all manner of goods from lace and lanterns to toys and tinsel, to go into the sideshows, to watch the clowns and acrobats, to listen to the fiddlers and drummers, to ride the swings and roundabouts. But most of all he longed to eat. The sight of other children licking penny ices or munching gingerbread or biting into pork pies made his own empty stomach rumble. But he needed money to buy food, and to get money he knew he had to work. 'All the fun of

14

the fair' was not for him and his family. They were there to make money, by their wits or by crime. And if they didn't, they faced a grim choice – starvation or the workhouse.

'Thanks for the tea, Liza. It's warmed my cockles,' said Cousin Annie, getting to her feet. 'Now I'd best be on my way. There're a load of sheep out there just waitin' to be fleeced,' she cackled, rubbing her hands in gleeful anticipation.

The Perkinskis split up then and set off on their day's work. Most of them were opportunists, begging or stealing whatever they could, but some were skilled workers and proud of it. Cousin Em was admired by the criminal community for her outstanding ability at picking pockets, her son Ted was following in his father Ernie's footsteps as a very promising forger of coins, Uncle Jack made a living with his blind-beggar dodge, Uncle Bill stole dogs and returned them to their grateful owners for a price and young Tom had taken his cousin Sam's place as the family's highly respected horse thief.

'What'll we do, Jem?' said Ned, who always looked to his older brother for a lead.

'Let's go and see the acrobats.'

'But we got to work. We got to get some money.'

'We will,' insisted Jem, 'after we've seen the acrobats.'

'But I want to see the performin' fleas,' said Billy. 'I want to see them pullin' tiny carts like they did last year.'

Jem was about to tell his little brother to shut up when he changed his mind and said with a sly grin, 'OK. But it'll cost you.'

'How much?'

'That farthin' you found in the gutter yesterday.'

Reluctantly Billy took the coin out of his pocket and handed it to his brother.

'Right you are,' said Jem. 'Here are the fleas.' And taking off his greasy wideawake hat, he thrust his dirty head in Billy's face.

Billy stared at it intently for a moment. 'I can see loads of fleas,' he said, 'but none of them are pullin' tiny carts.'

'Blimey, what d'you expect for a farthin'?' exclaimed Jem. 'See,' he held it up and winked at Ned, 'I already made some money.'

'That's not fair!' cried Billy, trying to snatch it back. 'That's not fair!'

'Stop larkin' around, you little varmints,' scolded their mother, overhearing the rumpus. 'Jem, take these cigars,' she said, giving him two boxes. 'See if you can get a penny a piece for them. And Ned, you carry these.' She gave him a tray with a few razors, bootlaces, corn plasters, nutmeg graters and sticks of sealing wax on it.

'Oh Ma, why do I always have to carry it?' he grumbled. 'Why can't Billy do it?'

'Cos he's too small.'

'But he never does nothin' except spoil all our dodges.'

'I could go with Gran and help her,' suggested Billy.

His grandmother frowned. 'I'll give you a penny to stay away from me.'

'If you give us twopence we'll all stay away from you,' said Jem hopefully.

'Enough of this clackin',' said Ma. 'Kate'll help Gran.'

'Nah, I won't,' retorted her daughter. 'I'm goin' to sing in the pubs. I've learned a whole lot of new songs, like "Sam Hall" and "The Mistletoe Bough" and "Jack Sheppard".'

'Let her do it, Liza,' said Gran. 'Soon as she opens her mouth they'll pay her to shut it.'

'Nah, she spends more time firkydoodlin' with the boys than workin'. You take her with you, Gran, so you can keep an eye on her,' said Ma firmly. 'And you three,' she turned to the boys, 'pack off! The sooner you get out there, the sooner you'll start earnin' some money.'

Although Jem had his cigars to sell, he kept his eyes open for the chance to remove a silk handkerchief, a watch, a snuff box or a wallet from the pocket of any unsuspecting person who didn't keep their wits about them. And there were plenty of people like that at the fair, many of them in from the country for the day and unused to the sharp ways of the London poor. But the competition was stiff. Gangs of thieves roamed the fairground, and Jem and Ned had to stay alert to protect their own property.

Ned urged everyone to buy his razors — 'Sharp as your wife's tongue!' he cried, while Billy trailed along behind him, whining, 'I'm hungry. I'm hungry.'

'Will you stop your caterwaulin'?' said Jem. 'We haven't got the ready to buy any grub.'

'But what about all the money them people gave you for the fight?' protested Billy.

'Pa took it.'

'What, the whole lot?'

'Yeh.'

'You could've kept some.'

'I tried but he tipped me upside down and it all fell out my pockets . . . Nah, wait a mo,' Jem said, his eyes lighting up, 'I just remembered I have got the ready.' And taking off one of his boots he pulled out a shiny new penny and held it up triumphantly.

'Where'd you get that?' said Ned.

'Uncle Ernie gave it me before they put him in clink.'

'Is it one of his specials?' giggled Billy, reaching for it.

'Yeh,' said Jem. 'Come on, let's go and toss the pieman.'

But Ned hung back, frowning. 'Nah, I don't think we should,' he said.

'You don't have to. But me and Billy're goin' to get a pie, biggest pie we can find,' said Jem, running off.

Ned hesitated for a moment, caught between his conscience — for he knew Uncle Ernie's coins were forgeries — and his stomach. There was a fierce tussle between the two. But when the stomach is so empty it hurts, the conscience has a hard time winning.

'Oy, wait for me!' he shouted, running after his brothers.

The pieman was easy to find because he was pushing his barrow round the fair and shouting at the top of his lungs, 'Here's all hot! Meat, fish or fruit! Toss or buy one! Up and win 'em!'

'Toss you for one, guv,' said Jem, running up to the man with the penny in his outstretched hand.

The pieman nodded. If he won the toss he would take Jem's penny without giving him a pie but if he lost he had to give Jem a pie for nothing. Many people tossed the pieman for the fun of it or because they couldn't resist a gamble and that way he made a lot more money than he would have done simply by selling them.

'Go on then,' he said to Jem.

Jem spun the coin high in the air and just before it fell to earth the pieman called out, 'Heads!'

'Lor', strike me lucky, it's tails,' chortled Jem. 'I'll have a hot eel pie, guv. Ned, why don't you have a go?' he said to his brother between mouthfuls.

Ned took the coin and tossed it in the air.

'Heads!' cried the pieman again.

'Nah, it's tails, guv,' said Ned. 'I'll have a mutton pie.' And he took one off the barrow and began devouring it.

'Go on, Billy,' said Jem. 'It's your turn.'

As Billy threw the coin in the air the pieman sang out 'Heads!' for a third time, but before the penny had even landed Billy said, 'Nah, it's tails,' and helped himself to a kidney pie.

The pieman narrowed his eyes and looked at him with deep suspicion. 'How did you know it was goin' to be tails?' he said.

'Cos . . . cos he knows what's goin' to happen,' said Jem quickly before Billy could answer. 'He's like my gran. She can tell the future cos she's a witch.'

'Well, I'm not, I'm a boy,' said Billy indignantly. 'And I knew it was goin' to be tails cos this penny's got tails on both sides. See,' he said, showing it to the pieman, 'it's a special one. Uncle Ernie makes them. That's why he's doin' five years' hard labour in clink.'

Jem gulped, Ned went white and the pieman, snatching the coin from Billy's hand, turned an interesting shade of purple.

'Why, you thievin' little . . .' he bellowed.

Jem grabbed Billy and the three boys set off as if the devil himself was at their heels. The angry pieman started to give chase, his face growing redder and redder, but he was uneasy about leaving his cart unattended and so, reluctantly, he turned back.

'You stupe!' stormed Jem, dragging Billy behind the Punch and Judy stand once they'd lost the irate pieman. 'Uncle Ernie made that penny special for me and now you've gone and given it away. Right, I'm goin' to . . .' But before he could give Billy a hearty whack, Ned grabbed his arm and pointed to a stout, prosperous-looking man with his wife and six children in tow.

'He looks like the kind of cove that'd buy your cigars,' he whispered.

'Yeh, you're right, he does look half baked,' agreed Jem with a wolfish grin. 'I reckon I'll get the ready off him quick as old boots . . . 'Scuse me, Your Honour,' he said, walking up to the man and raising his hat, 'could I interest you in some real plummy cigars, the very best money can buy? They come all the way from America.'

'All the way from America, eh?' The man raised his eyebrows in mock surprise. 'Then they must be very stale by now.' And he let out a great roar of laughter.

His wife and children laughed too, in an obedient way.

'Yeh, very comical,' said Jem. 'As a matter of fact my pa works at the East India Docks in London and he got them cigars off one of the boats.' He glanced over his shoulder frequently as if he was afraid of being overheard. Lowering his voice he went on, 'I wouldn't normally offer such a thunderin' bargain to anyone, but you look a very decent cove and I'd like to do you a favour.'

The man bent forward, his eyes glinting greedily, while his wife and children gathered round, straining to hear. 'Let's see them,' he whispered.

'I'll only get one out,' said Jem, still looking round furtively, 'just in case any of them customs men are around, cos if they see me sellin' them they'll cop me.' And opening one of the boxes he took out a handsome cigar with an impressive gold-leaf band around it.

The man took it from him and held it up to the light.

'Nice colour. Nice smell,' he said, putting it to his nose. 'Very good quality,' he added, rolling the cigar next to his ear. '"Real plummy,"' he laughed, 'just like you said.'

'Keep your voice down,' Jem pleaded. 'I've only got a few and if people find out how splendacious they are they'll go mad to get them.'

'How much do you want for them?' whispered the man.

'Well, I'll be straight with you, Your Worshipful,' said Jem, his face the very picture of honesty, 'my pa told me to sell them for threepence a piece but,' he smiled beguilingly, 'I'll let you have them for twopence a piece cos I've kind of taken to you. I think it must be cos you remind me of my dear old granpa who died.'

'Granpa didn't die,' said Billy. 'Gran says the old devil ran away with the barmaid at the Pig'n Whistle.'

'He was *run over* by the barmaid at the Pig'n Whistle,' said Jem, pulling Billy's cap down over his face to shut him up.

'*Run over by a barmaid?*' said the man incredulously.

'Yeh, she was drivin' one of them big brewery carts when my poor old granpa, who was blind as a rat, crossed the road and a wheel ran over him and cut him clean in two. They tried to stitch the two bits together again but—'

'It's blind as a bat,' said one of the girls.

'What is?' Jem frowned.

'You don't say "as blind as a rat." You say "as blind as a—"'

'Yes, yes, never mind about that,' her father interrupted. 'Look here, young fellow, I'll have a box of those cigars.' And he took a shilling from his wallet.

'God bless you, Your Nobleness,' said Jem, biting the coin to make sure it wasn't one of Uncle Ernie's and tucking it into the waistband of his trousers for safety. 'And I know my dear old granpa would say the same if he was here today in one piece,' he added with feeling. And, raising his wideawake, he walked away.

As soon as the man and his family were out of earshot Jem turned to his brothers and said, 'Right, quick, you two! Fast as you can before he opens the box.'

'Why?' cried Billy, trying to keep up with Jem and Ned as they sped away. 'What's wrong with the box?'

'It's got no cigars in it, leastwise not proper ones,' said Jem. 'They're just bits of brown paper rolled up and filled with sawdust. Ma and Cousin Annie made them last night.'

'What about the real cigar?' said Ned. 'You still got it?'

'Don't be soft. You don't think I'd give that away, do you?' scoffed Jem. 'And,' his dirty face broke into a grin, 'since Ma wanted me to sell the others for a penny apiece and I sold them to that dummy for twopence a piece, that means I've made . . .' He did a quick calculation on his fingers. 'I've made sixpence profit.'

Billy jumped up and down for joy. 'Now we can go'n see the performin' fleas,' he cried.

'Look, shut up about fleas,' snapped Jem. 'I'm not payin' good money to see somethin' I can see for nothin' on your head any time I want.'

'Nah, nor me,' agreed Ned. 'I want to see the fire-eaters.'

'And I want to see the wild-beast show,' said Jem.

So they went to the wild-beast show.

3

'Come on, Kate,' snapped Gran as her granddaughter trailed along behind her, smiling and winking at every boy she passed. 'If you don't get a move on I'll tell your 'Enry you've been flirtin' . . . Where is he, anyway? He should be here keepin' an eye on you, you hussy.'

'Don't be soft, Gran. He's a waterman, isn't he? This is the busiest time of the year for him. Him and his mate, Shep, are up and down the river all day, wherryin' folks back and forth to the fair. I reckon they'll make a fortune by the time it's over.'

'How much do they charge these days?'

'Sixpence when folks get in the boat. But when they get to the middle of the river Shep tells them it's a shillin' and if they don't like it they can get out and swim. My 'Enry doesn't agree with it, but Shep says it's the only way to make money.' Kate giggled.

'That Shep sounds like a clever bloke and no

flies,' said Gran admiringly. 'He's almost sharp enough to be a Perkinski.'

'But Henry's much nicer, Gran. And he paints.'

'Paints? What, walls, you mean?'

'Nah, pictures.'

'Pictures? Paff!' scoffed Gran. 'There's no money in that.'

'How much further are we goin'?' Kate complained. 'I'm done up carryin' this pesky sack. It's breakin' my back.'

'Over there.' Gran pointed to a vacant lot between groups of stilt-walkers and fire-eaters. 'I always set my stall there. And look –' she nudged Kate – 'they're all waitin' for me.'

It was true. A large crowd had gathered, eagerly awaiting the old lady's arrival. As soon as they caught sight of her a shout went up. 'There she is! There's Madam Natasha!' – for that was the name Gran used to sell her wares, although her real name was Doris.

'By jingo, you're lookin' stunnin', Madam Natasha,' chuckled a man as Gran staggered towards him in black satin shoes several sizes too small with holes cut out to ease her bunions.

'You're jammier than Queen Vic herself,' chortled another, running his eye over the old lady's long red skirt with row upon row of tatty frills half falling off, her moth-eaten shawl and bonnet with no crown.

'What've you got for us this year, Madam Natasha?' asked a woman, pressing forward eagerly as Gran set out her stall with a profusion of bottles, pots and jars full of brightly coloured potions and foul-smelling ointments.

'I've got somethin' real special,' replied Gran, holding up a phial of milky white liquid. 'Somethin' so splendiferous you'll never believe it.'

'You're right, I don't,' cried a wag at the back of the crowd.

'What's it called?' asked the woman, reaching for it, her eyes shining.

'Hocus-Pocus,' said the wag.

'It's called the Miracle of Life,' said Gran, ignoring him.

'Why's it called that?' asked the woman

'Cos if anyone's sappy enough to buy it, it'll be a miracle,' snorted the wag. And the crowd roared with laughter.

4

Jem and his brothers had no difficulty finding the wild-beast tent for it was covered with pictures of savage animals, blood dripping from their jaws. A man dressed in a splendid military uniform, sporting a huge waxed handlebar moustache and eyebrows to match, marched up and down outside, twirling a gold-topped cane and bellowing, 'Roll up! Roll up! Step inside to see the wild hanimals. They're so fierce they'd rip you limb from limb if they could. But have no fear, ladies'n gen'lemen, cos they're all safe behind bars.'

'This one . . .' he tapped with his cane a picture of a particularly ferocious lion, 'this here hanimal – you can see it inside for a penny ha'penny – has already eaten a dozen of its keepers. It chews off their heads and spits out their eyes,' he said, to cries of dismay and delight from the crowd.

'And this bear,' he tapped another picture, 'is known as a grizzly bear on account of it grizzles if it doesn't get enough human babies to eat. It bites a hole in their little necks and sucks out their blood like you and me drink lemonade.'

'And have you got a snake in there, guv?' piped up Billy.

The showman stepped back aghast, several women fainted, a man crossed himself, muttering a prayer, another clutched a lucky charm to his chest and Jem slapped a hand over his little brother's mouth.

'Hold your jaw, you stupe!' he hissed at him.

But it was too late. Everyone had heard.

'He said it. He said that word,' they whispered to each other, looking over their shoulders, their eyes wide with fear, for the Snake was the name the newspapers had given to a villain who was terrorizing London. In the previous six months there had been a spate of burglaries and muggings by a man who was clearly a maniac. Anyone who tried to protect their precious possessions had their throat slit or some other more hideous mutilation. The one or two who had survived his murderous onslaught, because some Good Samaritan had come to their aid, described him as a creature from the darkest swamp, half-man, half-reptile, his lidless eyes steeped in wickedness.

Every week there was news of yet another poor soul mercilessly slaughtered and in no time the superstition had taken root among the gullible that simply saying the murderer's name out loud was enough to attract the evil creature to their side, dagger in hand.

Fear quickly turned to anger and the crowd rounded on Billy for bringing such misfortune on their heads.

'Shut your trap, you little fool,' snapped a woman.

'Don't say that word again.'

'You'll get us all killed.'

'But,' Billy protested, 'I just wanted to know if there was a sna—'

'What's that funny-lookin' thing with a tail at both ends?' asked Jem quickly before his little brother could get them into trouble yet again.

'That, young fellow, is a helephant,' said the showman, who was equally keen to change the subject. 'The one we got — you can see it inside for a penny ha'penny — is the biggest helephant in the world. We had to knock three boats into one just to bring it over here from America where helephants run wild. And horrible fierce it is too. With its trunk — this here is its trunk,' he pointed to it, 'it can pick

32

up a grown man, swing him round and round its head and throw him right over the rooftops. I seen it with my own eyes, ladies'n gen'lemen,' he said, as the crowd gasped. 'I seen one of them dreadful creatures throw a man so far that when he landed he was in a different country.'

Everyone, including Jem, Ned and Billy, eagerly gave up their pennies to see such terrifying animals. But once inside the hot, stuffy tent they were sadly disappointed. In the first cage was a moth-eaten old bear with the saddest expression in its rheumy eyes. The second cage housed 'the biggest helephant in the world', only someone must have left it out in the rain because it had shrunk to a very small, skinny thing with barely the strength to swing its trunk, let alone hurl a man over the rooftops with it. And a tired, toothless old lion, its mangy coat covered in scabs and scars, lay sleeping in the far corner of the third cage.

'Crikey, I seen fiercer cats than that in Devil's Acre,' complained Ned.

'We paid good money to see it eatin' its keepers and all it's doin' is sleepin',' said Jem angrily. 'Why don't you wake it up, Ned?'

'Not me,' Ned said, backing away in alarm. 'I'm not goin' in that cage.'

'Wake it up with your catapult, you block'ead!'

'Oh yeh, right,' said Ned, pulling the stick from his pocket. 'Find a stone . . . Not a round one, Billy,' he said as the little boy rooted around on the ground. 'I want somethin' sharp.'

'Here's a crack one,' said Jem. 'That should liven it up.'

Ned loaded the catapult and took aim, but the stone missed the lion by a yard. It pinged off the bars of its cage and ricocheted into the mouth of a woman who was standing nearby, gawping at the beast. She swallowed, choked, turned blue and sank to the ground, gasping.

'I think we'd better go,' muttered Jem. 'She looks like she's snuffed it.'

As the three boys ran out of the tent they collided with their mother and Cousin Annie, who were trying to sell the daffodils and tulips they'd stolen.

'What were you doin' in there?' demanded Ma. 'You weren't workin', that's for sure.'

'We were,' protested Jem. 'We were just . . . er . . . just seein' if any of them wanted a cigar.'

'What, the wild animals? Don't tell me the lions have taken up smokin'?'

'I've already sold one box, Ma,' said Jem.

At that his mother's face softened. 'Well done, my precious,' she said. 'I always knew you were a . . .'

But Jem never found what Ma always knew he was because Cousin Annie cried, 'Hey up! Somethin's happenin'!' as a crowd of people rushed out of the tent, chattering excitedly.

'What's up, missus!' she asked, grabbing one of them by the arm.

'Woman in there . . . Terrible tragedy . . . Standin' by the lion's cage mindin' her own business,' babbled the woman. 'Lion asleep . . . Next thing, it leaps up and bites her head clean off.'

'Where's her head now?' asked Cousin Annie.

'In the lion, of course.'

'It won't want no supper then,' said Ma.

'They're bringin' her out,' the shout went up. 'Stand back!'

Immediately everyone pressed forward, craning their necks.

'Here, let's take a look,' said Ma, elbowing her way to the front of the crowd. 'I've never seen a headless woman before.' But her face fell as the woman was carried past on a plank of wood. 'Nah,' she shouted to Cousin Annie, 'there's nothin' to see. She's still got her head on but she's clutchin' her throat. I reckon she must've swallowed somethin' small and sharp like a . . .' She suddenly caught sight of the catapult dangling from Ned's hand and stopped mid-sentence. 'Ned?' she cried, a suspicious look on her face. 'Give me that catapult, you little . . . !' But before she could catch them, Ned, Jem and Billy had gone.

5

Some months earlier, on a dark, rainy night, an elderly man by the name of Charles Sterling was walking down Upper St Martin's Lane, a busy road close to Seven Dials, when he encountered Flo Forbes – collided with her, to be more precise, for she ran out of a side alley and barged into him.

'Beggin' your pardon, guv,' she said. And drawing a tattered shawl closely around her head and shoulders, she ran across the road. But the cobblestones were wet and covered with manure and she lost her footing and, with a cry of anguish, fell heavily.

'My dear lady . . . Here, let me help you,' said Mr Sterling, holding out his hand.

'I can't get up, guv,' she gasped. 'It's my ankle. I think it's broke.'

'We must get you to a hospital.'

'Nah! Nah! Not a hospital. I'm not goin' there!'

she cried in alarm. 'Nobody never comes out of one of them alive.'

'But that ankle needs attention.'

'I'll be all right, guv. I just need to get home.'

It was obvious from her determined expression that Mr Sterling was never going to persuade the woman to get medical help, and so, reluctantly, he helped her to her feet.

'Where is your home?' he asked.

'That way, guv.' She pointed. 'Church Street.'

Church Street was in the heart of Seven Dials, a notorious slum teeming with criminals of every kind from area thieves to cut-throats. There were murmurings and mutterings as Mr Sterling helped the limping woman through the squalid alleyways and dingy courtyards and once or twice a dark shape loomed over them menacingly, only to disappear with a, 'Oh, it's you, Flo. Sorry, my tulip' – for while the slum dwellers thought nothing of maiming and murdering a stranger, they seldom harmed their own.

'This is where I live, guv,' said the woman, stopping in front of a cheap lodging house with no door and pieces of cardboard and old rags covering the windows. 'I'll be all right now,' she said, letting go of his arm and starting to climb the steep, narrow staircase. But her ankle gave way and she fell back, wincing.

'On which floor is your room?' asked Mr Sterling.

'Top one, sir,' said the woman, who had turned deathly pale. 'Three flights up.'

Although Charles Sterling was an elderly man he was still strong, while Flo Forbes, who was a young woman, was weak and undernourished. She weighs no more than a child, Mr Sterling thought, as he lifted her and carried her up the stairs, treading carefully lest he plunge his foot through the rotting wood.

Rats skittered over his feet, cockroaches climbed the walls and once he trod on the decomposing body of a cat. But worse was to come when he reached the room that Flo Forbes shared with nine or ten other men and women. For a moment Mr Sterling thought the stench from their unwashed bodies would choke him and he almost slipped and fell in the foul-smelling overflow from the slop bucket in the middle of the room in which everyone relieved themselves.

At sight of the woman in his arms, a small girl shot to her feet and ran towards them, crying, 'Mum! Mum! What's wrong? Are you ill?'

'Your mother has broken her ankle,' said Mr Sterling.

'Broke it? Oh Lor',' she exclaimed. 'Now what'll we do?'

Mr Sterling looked at the other tenants of the room, tramps mostly, huddled together on the filthy floorboards in various degrees of drunkenness. 'Is that your brother or sister?' he said to the girl, nodding at a baby sleeping in a pile of rags in the corner.

'My brother, Pip.'

'And what is your name, child?'

The girl looked up at him with bright button eyes. 'Clara,' she said. 'My name's Clara Forbes.'

A look of infinite sadness passed over Mr Sterling's face and he appeared to be struggling to control some strong emotion.

'What's wrong, guv?' Clara frowned. 'Don't you like it?'

'On the contrary, my dear, I think it is the most beautiful name in the world. It is the name I gave my baby daughter who died many years ago, long before you were born,' he said with a wistful smile. 'And now may I suggest you pick up your little brother, Clara, and follow me.'

'Where you takin' us, guv?' said Flo Forbes in

alarm, as he carried her back down the rickety stairs. 'I'm not goin' to no hospital. I already told you. I'm not goin' . . .'

'Calm yourself, dear lady,' said Mr Sterling. 'I am taking you home.'

'But this is our home,' said Clara, perplexed.

'But there is no one here to care for your mother, Clara. My housekeeper is a good, kind lady and she will look after her, and you and little Pip too, until your mother is strong and well again.'

In his youth Charles Sterling had inherited a modest amount of money from his father, which he had invested in a small carriage-building business in Long Acre. With determination and hard work he had built it up over the years until he had sufficient money to marry and move his bride into a mid-terrace house in Victoria Square, a peaceful location close to Buckingham Palace. From his drawing-room window he looked out on pleasant gardens set with evergreen trees, shrubs and flowers. But within two years of his wedding Mr Sterling's happiness was shattered when his wife and baby died in child-birth and from then on he lived quite alone, save for a housekeeper and two maids.

Mr Sterling found solace in his work and in time

he took on a partner, an ambitious young man called Septimus Mallick, who raised the business to new heights. Carriages made by Sterling & Mallick Ltd could be seen all over London, their handsome exteriors covered with finest leather painted in rich colours, their elegant interiors lined with silk and fine cloth. A Sterling & Mallick carriage invariably bore the coat of arms of an illustrious family on its door and was pulled by two or four perfectly matched horses, their heads held high, their coats gleaming.

Mr Sterling refrained from using any of his carriages, however. Six mornings a week, whatever the weather, he could be seen striding from his Victoria Square home to his place of work in Long Acre and back again at night, a considerable journey even for a much younger man.

'It keeps me fit, you see,' he explained to anyone who asked. 'Keeps my brain active too, for I look and listen and learn as I walk through the streets of this fine city.'

It also kept his pockets empty, because he never went anywhere without a quantity of coins which he distributed to the unfortunates he met on his way. So Mrs Restall, his long-suffering housekeeper, was hardly surprised when she saw the hansom cab draw up and Mr Sterling get out with the stricken woman and her two children.

'More waifs and strays,' she said to Rose, one of the housemaids. 'How many times have we had to nurse some pauper back to health?'

'More times than I can remember, Mrs Restall,' laughed Rose. 'But you're just like the master. You love helping them as much as he does.'

'I don't get the choice, girl. I do what I'm told. I'm only a servant here.'

'You're more than a servant in the master's eyes, Mrs Restall. How long have you been with him . . . ? Thirty years? You're more like old friends.'

'Well, this old friend is going to have her work cut out with them.' The housekeeper nodded at Clara, who was clambering up the steps with Pip in her arms. 'Go and let them in, Rose, and I'll tell Maisie to prepare the guests' bedrooms – again,' she said, shaking her head in mock despair.

Clara had never slept in a bed before, never worn pretty clothes, never eaten a proper meal. For the first few days in Mr Sterling's house she was so overcome she wandered from room to room running her fingers over the damask curtains, the silk cushions, the highly polished tables, the myriad ornaments and vases and lamps as if she was in some kind of wonderland. Often she pinched herself so hard it hurt. Then she knew she hadn't died and gone to some heavenly place like the preachers in the streets were always talking about.

Thanks to Mr Sterling's excellent doctor, Flo Forbes's ankle healed quickly. Much too quickly for Clara, who didn't want to leave her lovely new home. 'Oh Ma,' she pleaded, 'couldn't you break the other one?'

The ankle healed far too quickly for Mr Sterling as well. In the short time the little family had been there he had grown very fond of them. Every morning he left for work a little later so that he could stay and have breakfast with them and, if the weather was good, take a stroll in the park, leading Clara by the hand while a nursemaid carried young Pip. Every evening he came home a little earlier so he could play with the children before dinner and sit with their mother afterwards, talking and laughing as if they were an old married couple. And deep in his heart that was what Mr Sterling wanted, for as her health improved Flo Forbes's frail body began to fill out and she blossomed into a pretty woman with a sweet nature and gentle manner.

'There'll be wedding bells soon, Mrs Restall,' giggled Rose. 'I can almost hear them.'

'Don't be impertinent, girl,' snapped the house-keeper. And then her face softened. 'But I reckon you're right. I never thought I'd live to see the day the master took a new wife. He's been so lonely all these years, his life has been nothing but work, work, work. He deserves some happiness at last.'

'But she's not his class.' Rose shook her head doubtfully. 'What will his friends say, him taking a woman from the streets?'

'When has Mr Sterling ever cared what other people say?' retorted the housekeeper indignantly. 'He loves her. And I can tell from the way she looks at him she feels the same way. And then there are the children. He thinks the world of young Pip. And as for Clara,' she smiled, 'she's the little girl he lost all those years ago.'

And so Clara's wish was granted. Mr Sterling married her mother, adopted the children and the house in Victoria Square became their home. Her new father was a kind man, who did his utmost to make his new family happy. He was also very pro-tective of them, especially Clara, for he was old enough and wise enough to know that there were many wicked people on the streets of London who thought nothing of harming children for their own gain.

'Look after my little daughter. Never let her out of your sight,' he instructed the governess he had hired to look after Clara. 'Guard her with your life.'

6

The most popular booth at Greenwich fair was the freak show. But it cost a penny each to get in, and Jem had only a penny ha'penny left.

'Strictly speakin' it's mine cos I was the one that sold that bloke them cigars,' Jem said, 'so I'll go in and you two can wait outside.'

'If you go in without us I'll tell Ma you sold them for twopence a piece and spent the rest,' growled Ned.

'You wouldn't dare, knocker-face!'

'Try me, cabbage 'ead!'

'Billy, take Ned's tray,' said Jem. 'Him and me are goin' to have a bit of a chat. We'll be back in a kick.' And disappearing behind the nearest bushes, the two boys set about each other with fists and feet.

'So it's settled then,' said Ned, spitting out a tooth. 'You're not goin' in the freak show without Billy and me.'

'All right,' agreed Jem, wiping his bloody nose on the sleeve of his coat. 'I know how we can all get in without payin'.'

'What're you goin' to do?' asked Ned nervously.

'Don't worry, we won't end up in clink. Come on, let's go and get Billy.'

But Billy had disappeared.

'Where's that little varmint got to?' said Jem. 'We've only been gone a couple of minutes.'

'There.' Ned pointed. 'He's over there with the baked-potato man.'

'What's he doin'? He hasn't got no money to buy any.'

'Course he hasn't. But you know Billy – next to scorfin' grub he likes lookin' at it.'

Their laughter turned to amazement, however, when Billy held up a coin to the man, who reached into a brightly polished can, took out a hot potato, spread some creamy yellow butter on it, sprinkled it with salt and handed it to the little boy.

'Where d'you get the ready to buy *that*?' demanded Jem, running over to him.

'A bloke gave it me,' said Billy, his cheeks bulging.

'A bloke?'

'Yeh.'

'Why?'

'Cos I sold him Ma's tray.'

'What, the whole lot?' Ned could scarcely believe his ears. Sometimes it took a week or more to persuade people to buy all the bits and pieces Ma hawked around the streets from early morning to late at night. And to sell the tray in five minutes flat was an amazing achievement. 'Lor', that's stunnin', Billy. You must've got a pretty penny for it.'

'I did.' Billy grinned, his mouth full of hot potato.

'How much d'you get?'

'A penny, like you said.'

Ned opened his mouth to say something, but all that came out was a strange, strangled sound that sounded vaguely like 'Blimey!'

'But I haven't got the penny no more,' explained Billy, 'cos I bought this with it.' And he swallowed the last of the potato.

His face bright red with anger, Ned lunged at the little boy, fists flailing, shouting, 'You stupe! You gibfaced, half-baked, addlepated cod's head! I'm goin' to . . .!'

But before Ned could grab him, Billy dodged behind Jem and clung to him for protection.

'It's no use cryin' over spilt beer,' said Jem philosophically as Ned cursed and moaned at his little brother. 'The tray's gone and there's nothin' you can do about it.'

'But Ma'll give me the back of her hand when she finds out,' whined Ned, cringing at the prospect.

'You're right,' agreed Jem. 'And she'll give you the front of her boot too. But you might as well enjoy yourself before you die, so let's go to the freak show. You and Billy stand over there,' he pointed to a spot well away from the entrance to the tent, 'and wait till I give you the signal.' And he sauntered up to the woman who was sitting behind a table selling tickets, lifted his wideawake and said, "Scuse me, missus, I wonder if I could interest you in this?'

He held up the remaining cigar box.

Since there was nobody waiting to go into the freak show at that moment and she had nothing better to do, the woman decided to humour the cheeky urchin.

'I don't smoke cigars,' she said. 'I prefer a pipe.'

'Nah, there are no cigars in it.'

'Oh, so you're sellin' me an empty box, are you?'

'It's not empty. There's a black widow in it.'

'A black widow? Now how did you get a poor widow woman in a little box like that? Chopped her arms and legs off, did you?' said the ticket seller, slapping her thigh and chuckling hugely at her own joke.

'It isn't a woman,' said Jem. 'A black widow's a spider, a thumpin' great big 'un. It's a bit squashed in. I should've put it in a bigger box. I hope it's all right.' He lifted the lid the merest fraction and peered inside. 'Yeh, it's still alive,' he said. 'In fact, it's fightin' to get out. It's got a kind of mad look in its eyes, like it wants to sink its teeth into someone.'

The woman turned deathly pale. 'Where did you get such a horrible thing?' she gasped.

'My pa. He's a soldier; he goes all round the world fightin'. And he always brings us back plummy presents. He got this thumpin' great spider in Scotland — that's near Australie — but we don't want it cos we already got dozens of dogs and cats and—'

'And I don't want it neither,' said the woman. 'Go on, you little varmint!' she cried in a shrill voice, waving Jem away.

'Wouldn't you like to have a look at it, missus?' suggested Jem, smiling sweetly. 'I reckon you'll change your mind. It'd make a jammy pet. It's all black and hairy with big, fat legs. You could take it for walks. But you mustn't stroke it,' he added, wagging a warning finger, 'cos it'll bite you. Then your body'll swell up and go all stiff and you'll die a horrible death, foamin' at the mouth and . . .'

'Fluff it, I said! Take it away!'

'Just take a quick look,' insisted Jem, moving round the table towards her, 'cos I'm sure you'll want it when you see it. You'll probably grow to love it in time, if it doesn't kill you first. Here it is . . . Oops!' he cried, pretending to trip over one of the guy ropes that supported the tent. 'Oh crimes, I've dropped the plaguy box and the spider's got out. Pa'll give me a right wallopin' if it gets away.'

'Help!' The woman screamed and leaped to her feet, overturning her chair. 'Help!'

'Don't panic, missus!' cried Jem, scrabbling around on his hands and knees under the table. 'Don't panic. I'll find it in a . . . Oh good, there it is. I can see it.'

'Where? Where?'

'It's gone up your skirt.'

With a piercing shriek the woman took to her heels.

When she was safely out of sight, Jem picked up the cigar box, put it in his pocket, waved to his brothers and the three of them went into the freak show.

7

The tent was made of canvas so thick that the interior was hot and dark. Jem, Ned and Billy, coming in from the brilliant sunlight of a spring morning, had to stand still for a moment or two. As their eyes grew accustomed to the gloom they made out a row of gas-lit booths, each separated from the other by a flimsy wall. In every booth was a raised platform and a chair or bed on which sat or lay one of the freaks, while the crowd ambled past, gawping at them and making tactless remarks.

In the first was the 'Prehistoric Man', a fearsome creature with wild eyes and sharp fangs, dressed in a lion's skin. A sign above his head informed the crowd: 'Before he was captured in a long and ferocious fight, this man lived for thousands of years in a cave way up in the mountains. He is the last prehistoric man to walk the earth.' In one hand he had a club, which he waved menacingly, causing several women to faint, and in the other he held what appeared to be the leg of a very large animal, which he gnawed greedily.

'That a beef bone, guv?' called Billy, his mouth watering.

The caveman grunted.

'I said is that a—'

'Don't be sappy,' said a woman standing next to Billy. 'He's a caveman, isn't he? He can't speak. Not English, anyway.'

'Where did he get that bone from? Did he get it from a butcher's shop?'

'You're a right ninny, you are,' the woman laughed. 'They didn't have butchers' shops in them days. They dug big holes outside their caves and wild animals came along and fell in and the cavemen killed them . . .'

'And took them to the baker's, like people take their meat and potatoes of a Sunday to be cooked,' said Jem knowledgeably. 'And the baker put them in his oven and roasted them till they were crisp and juicy.'

Billy's face lit up. 'Why don't we do that?' he said. 'Why don't we dig a big hole outside our caravan in Devil's Acre and . . .'

'Oh, stow it, Billy!' retorted Jem.

The 'Man Mountain' was almost seven foot tall

with muscles that bulged like balloons. While the boys watched, open-mouthed, he picked up an iron cannonball and carried it round his booth, balancing it on one finger as if it was no heavier than a feather.

'Blimey!' breathed Jem. 'I reckon he's stronger than Pa.'

The 'Bearded Lady' was even more spectacular. Although she had a very handsome moustache and whole bushes growing out of her nose and ears, it was her beard that caused the crowd to cry, 'Lawks a mercy!' As thick as a privet hedge , it flowed over her chest and stomach and spread out on the floor around her like a carpet.

'How long did it take you to grow that, missus?' asked Ned.

'A couple of days.' She shrugged. 'If I didn't cut it, it'd stretch from here to London Bridge.'

The 'Woman with Two Heads' was disappointing. One of her heads seemed lively enough. It talked and laughed and drank a glass of gin and hot water, but the other lolled on her shoulder like a rag doll's. And the Dancing Dog was in a sulk and refused to budge from its bed.

In the last booth was the Pirate. He had a black patch over one eye, a wooden leg and a vicious hook where his right hand should have been. A brilliantly coloured parrot perched on his shoulder and he and the bird engaged in lively banter, to the amusement of Jem, Ned and Billy who pushed their way to the front of the crowd to watch.

'Yo ho ho!' cried the Pirate. 'Twenty fathoms deep on a dead man's chest.'

'Leave off!' screeched the bird. 'Leave off, timber toes.'

'Yo ho ho and a bottle of—'

'Whisky.'

'Rum. It's not whisky, you stupid bird, it's—'

'Pack off!'

'And who d'you think you're tellin' to pack off? Another word out of you, you moth-eaten, mangy-lookin' creature and I'll pull your feathers out one by one and have you for dinner.'

'Mud in your eye!'

This was the cue for the Pirate to put his hand under his eye patch, take out his eye, pop it in his mouth with a wicked grin and swallow it.

'Naughty boy,' squawked the parrot, dancing up and down. 'Naughty boy.'

'Father, did that man really eat his own eye?' asked a little girl.

'No, my dear, he was only pretending. And,' the

man lowered his voice, 'it was almost certainly a glass eye. He has hidden it in his mouth.'

'So he's cheatin',' laughed the girl.

Jem turned round, his eyes searching the crowd. He recognized that laugh, that voice. It sounded like Clara Forbes, the crossing sweeper who had escaped from the workhouse with him and his brothers, but in the dim light he couldn't see anyone like the girl he knew, in her shabby clothes and pieces of string looped through holes in her ears. The only girl standing nearby, holding her father's hand, was beautifully dressed in a pink ruched silk bonnet, a coat of finest cotton, button-up boots in soft leather and white kid gloves, her auburn hair brushed into gleaming ringlets around her face.

Jem stared at her. There was something about her – the bright button eyes, the confident, almost defiant tilt of the chin, but . . . Nah, he thought, it can't be Clara, not dressed like that, not with that toff.

But at that moment she turned her head, met his eye and exclaimed, 'Jem!'

'Blimey,' Jem said. 'It is you, Clara. What're you doin' in that gear? Did you nick it?'

'Course I didn't.' Clara laughed. 'Father,' she said

to the man, 'this is the boy I told you about, the one that got us out of the Strand Workhouse.'

'Not Jem Perkinski?' said an elegantly dressed woman appearing at her side.

'That's right, Mum,' said Clara. 'And it was his father who came to see us when we lived in Seven Dials and gave us all that golopshus grub.'

'Delicious food, Clara,' said her father in a quiet voice.

'Sorry, Father – delicious food.'

'Well, your father was very kind to us, Jem,' said Clara's mother, 'and I'd like to repay him by givin' you . . .' But just as Clara's mother was about to open her reticule and give Jem some money a tall, thin man strode up, lifted his top hat and said, 'Mr and Mrs Sterling, what a pleasure to see you. Did I not tell you you would find the most splendid pirate here?'

'I am most obliged to you, Septimus,' said Mr Sterling to his business partner. 'I confess this kind of entertainment is not to my taste, but my wife has never been to Greenwich fair and when my daughter heard there was a real, live pirate,' he looked fondly at Clara, 'she insisted on coming.'

'It's cos my Uncle Bob's a pirate,' she explained.

'Your uncle is a sailor, my dear,' laughed Mr Sterling. 'I do not think he would take kindly to being called a criminal.'

'Come, sir,' said Septimus Mallick, taking Mr Sterling by the arm, 'allow me to entertain you and Mrs Sterling to some refreshment. I know of a most pleasing hostelry, the Trafalgar. It is by the water's edge.'

'That is most kind of you, Septimus. I confess all this walking has given me a healthy appetite,' said Mr Sterling. And the three of them began to move away, chatting amiably.

'That's not your real pa, is it, Clara?' asked Jem, who had lingered behind, curious to hear more about Clara's amazing turn of fortune.

'Nah, he croaked – I mean, died – years ago. This one's my new father. He's dirty rich. We live in a posh house and we eat proper grub – food – and wear jammy togs – nice clothes – and we got servants. Pip, my little brother, has his own nursemaid and I've got a governess, a nice lady called Miss Graham. She was supposed to come with us today but she's got the molly grubs – I mean, a stomach ache – so she had to stay home.'

'Lor', you struck it lucky, Clara,' said Jem.

'Yeh, we did.'

'Pity we didn't.'

 59

'What d'you mean?'

'Your ma was just goin' to give us some of the ready when that poxy bloke came up.'

'I'll give you somethin', Jem,' said Clara. 'I haven't got none of the ready – I mean, money – but you can have these.' She took off her bonnet and gloves and pulled a silk scarf from her pocket and gave them to him.

'Lor', thanks,' said Jem, running his grubby fingers over the rich fabrics. 'They're real jammy. Our ma'll get a few bob for them at the market.'

'Clara, come along, my dear,' her father called to her.

'Comin', Dad,' she called back, lingering for a moment longer to watch the Pirate take out his glass eye again and give it to the parrot.

'He swallowed it! He did! The bird swallowed it!' Clara cried, clapping her hands.

'Would you like to hold Joey, little girl?' said the man.

'Oh, could I?'

'Stand quite still and I'll put him on your shoulder. There,' the man said as the parrot gently nibbled Clara's ear, 'he likes you.'

'What does he eat?'

60

'Apples are his favourite. I've got one here. You can give him some, if you like.'

'Oh yes. Yes, I would,' said Clara, excitedly.

'Make sure you don't get your fingers too near his beak,' said the man, cutting a small apple into pieces, 'cos if you do . . . Now what's up?' He frowned, for there was a sudden ruckus outside the tent.

'It's one of the acrobats,' shouted a woman who had run out to see what was happening. 'He's fallen off the tightrope. I think he's broken his leg . . . No, he's broken both legs.'

In an instant everybody followed her, pushing and shoving each other to get a better view of the catastrophe.

Jem, Ned and Billy ran too, but in the crush Jem was knocked down. Unaware of the boy lying on the ground, several people trod on him. By the time he clambered to his feet, bruised and cursing, the tent was empty, save for Clara, who was still feeding pieces of apple to the parrot on her shoulder. But just as Jem turned to go he heard a stifled scream and, glancing back, he saw a man with a hideous face, the face of an animal, a reptile, he could hardly tell what in the flickering gaslight, pounce on the little girl and carry her away. The parrot flew back to its master, squawking angrily, and the two of them disappeared, melting into the shadows.

Jem was rooted to the spot, scarcely believing what he had seen. Before he had regained his senses the crowd came back into the tent, grumbling loudly that nobody had fallen off the tightrope, it had been a hoax, and if they ever got their hands on the woman who had tricked them . . .

Jem saw Clara's mother and father looking anxiously about them and calling, 'Clara, where are you? Clara!' He started towards them to tell them what he'd seen, but as luck – or bad luck – would have it, the man to whom Jem had sold the fake cigars came into the tent at that moment and catching sight of Jem he shouted, 'There he is! There's the little varmint who cheated me.'

Hearing the fuss, the woman selling tickets came in to find out what was happening and seeing Jem she cried out, 'He cheated me too. Got in for nothin', he did. Told me a right whopper about a thunderin' great spider, the little varmint.'

'And he's got my girl's bonnet and gloves, and her neckerchief too,' gasped Clara's mother.

'He must've nicked them from her, missus,' said the ticket seller. 'He's a rogue – you can see it in his eyes. He'll stop at nothin' to get what he wants.'

'Where is she? Where's my little girl?' Flo cried, a note of panic entering her voice.

'I reckon he knows where she is. What've you done to her, eh, you little rascal?'

Jem knew he was in serious trouble. It was bad enough that he had sold fake cigars and tricked his way into the freak show, for which he would certainly be put in prison, but now he was suspected of kidnapping a rich man's daughter. And for that he could be hanged. It was pointless to stay and protest that he was innocent. He couldn't prove it, and they wouldn't believe him. He would be arrested and taken before a magistrate and he'd been there too often before and knew what that meant . . . No, no, he had to get away. And before anyone could stop him he barged through the crowd, dodging this way and that, avoiding outstretched hands.

'After him!' they shouted, giving chase. 'Stop that boy! Stop him!'

7

Clara felt as if she was in the grip of a powerful snake, its coils wrapped round her body, choking her. In vain she struggled to free herself as she was carried into darkness.

'Help!' she cried, breaking free for one brief moment. 'Help!' But a cold, damp hand was clamped over her mouth, silencing her screams.

'Keep quiet,' a man hissed in her ear. 'Keep quiet or . . .'

The grip around her tightened until she could barely breathe.

8

Ned and Billy watched in horror as Jem sped away with the crowd in hot pursuit.

'Come on,' Ned said, grabbing Billy's hand. 'Run! We got to find Pa and tell him what's happened.'

'But Pa's fightin' Amen the Assin.'

'Nah, he'll be in the Black Boy and Cat by now, celebratin' . . . Come on, we've got to get to him before he gets too drunk to help us.'

But when they got to the pub their father was nowhere to be seen.

''Scuse me, guv,' Ned said to a man coming out. 'D'you know what happened at the big fight?'

'What big fight?'

'The one between Bert the Beast and Ahmed the Assassin.'

'There was no fight, son. Bert the Beast tripped over the ropes just as he was gettin' into the ring, fell flat on his mug and broke his nose and three ribs.'

'Crimes, where is he now?' cried Ned in alarm.

'In hospital. And as far as I'm concerned, he can stay there. Bert the Beast? Paff!' The man exclaimed in a voice ringing with contempt. 'More like Bert the Booby if you ask me. Waste of money, waste of good money,' he muttered, walking away.

'Oh drat!' Ned exclaimed in frustration. 'If only Jem was here now.'

'If Jem was here now we wouldn't be lookin' for Pa,' said Billy with a rare flash of insight.

'I know that, you ninny. I only meant . . .' He only meant that although they spent most of their time arguing and fighting, he felt quite bereft without his brother, for they had never been apart for any length of time. Jem's audacity frequently got them into difficult situations, but his quick wit always got them out and the thought of Jem spending years in prison or transported to a faraway country was too bleak to contemplate.

'Let's find Ma,' said Billy. 'She'll know what to do.'

'Ma'll be workin'. And where'll we find her in this lot?' said Ned, looking despairingly at the vast crowd thronging the fairground. 'I think the whole of London's here today.'

'Look, there's Uncle Jack.' Billy pointed. 'Over there, with his mutt. He'll help us.'

'Yeh,' said Ned eagerly. 'Come on.'

Uncle Jack was having a very unsuccessful day. He was doing his blind-beggar dodge and Bella, his bulldog, was not helping one bit. He had trained her to stop whenever anyone showed the slightest interest in them, but on that Easter Monday Bella was suffering from a severe attack of spring fever. While Uncle Jack was on the prowl for money, Bella was on the lookout for a mate. At the sight of a male dog, any male, no matter how miserable or mangy, her stump of a tail wagged furiously.

To her delight a one-eyed mongrel with well-chewed ears and half a tail came shuffling over to present his compliments. Bella stopped, eyeing her suitor coyly, and Uncle Jack, thinking that the bulldog had met a generous person with a sympathetic ear, immediately went into his patter.

'Spare a coin for a blind man, guv. I lost my sight in the war fightin' for Queen and country,' he whined, fluttering his eyelids to try to catch a glimpse of the person listening to his tragic story. 'Anythin' you can spare, missus, any coin, however small, will be used to feed me and my poor starvin' family.' And he stretched out his hand, the palm cupped, to receive what he hoped would be a generous donation. But nothing happened.

'And, of course, I'd use some of your money to feed my faithful dog,' he continued, hoping he had come upon a lover of animals. 'She's the best friend a man can have,' he added, reaching down to pat Bella's head. 'Been with me through thick and thin, that dog has. I wouldn't part with her for nothin'. Give generously, guv or missus, so's I can buy a few crumbs for her and me,' he pleaded, putting out his hand again. Usually this tug at the heart strings was good for a few coins. But still nothing happened.

After a minute or two, when he hoped nobody was watching, Uncle Jack opened one eye the merest fraction, for it was a crime to cheat the public by feigning blindness and he knew he would be severely punished if caught.

To his dismay he discovered that he was standing quite alone, wasting his piteous pleas on thin air while Bella and her new friend circled each other. Uncle Jack gave his 'faithful dog' a swift kick in the ribs and waved her admirer away with his stick. He was none too pleased either when Ned and Billy ran up, babbling ten to the dozen.

'You've got to help us, Uncle Jack.'

'We were in the freak show . . .'

'Watchin' the Pirate . . .'

'And a woman said somebody'd fallen off the tightrope . . .'

'And broke both their legs . . .'

'And we all went to look . . .'

'Only it wasn't true, worse luck . . .'

'And when we got back . . .'

'Jem was . . .'

'Cut it, you two!' snapped Uncle Jack. 'Can't you see I'm workin'? And you should be too, instead of playin' sappy games. Pirate, indeed! Tightrope, paff! Load of bosh!'

'We're not playin' games, we're not, Jem's in trouble,' cried Ned, his voice rising hysterically.

'Jem's always in trouble.'

'But this is different. This is real trouble.' Ned tugged at his uncle's arm.

'I keep tellin' you I'm workin'. I haven't got the time to . . .'

'But you've you got to,' insisted Billy, pushing him from behind.

The three of them made such a commotion that a crowd began to gather, pointing and murmuring.

'What're them boys doin'?'

'They're attackin' that poor blind beggar.'

'They're tryin' to steal his money.'

'Shame! Leave him alone, you little varmints, or we'll have the law on you.'

'Police! Police!'

'Now see what you've done,' Uncle Jack hissed. And before the three of them could run away a constable arrived, swinging his truncheon ominously.

'What's all this, then?' he demanded.

'Them boys are toolers,' explained a helpful person in the crowd.

'We're not pickpockets,' said Ned indignantly. 'We were just . . . we were just havin' a bit of fun.'

'Fun? You call it fun beatin' a helpless blind man, do you?'

'We weren't . . .'

'Nah, we weren't,' said Billy. 'He's our Uncle Jack and we were tryin' to get him to help us find—'

'Some grub, cos we're hungry,' Ned cut in quickly, scowling at Billy, for a Perkinksi would never tell the police the truth.

'Are these boys your nephews, sir?' asked the policeman, turning to Uncle Jack.

'I can't say for sure, constable, cos I can't see them. I been stone blind since birth. But they do sound like Ned and Billy – they're my brother Bert's boys.'

'Perhaps you could describe them for me, sir, just

to be sure they are who they say they are and not common or garden thieves, of which there is a great number in the fairground today,' said the policeman, to nodded agreement and murmurs of disgust from the crowd.

'Well, sir,' said Uncle Jack, trying to be as polite and obliging as he could in the hope the constable would go away, 'Ned, he's the biggest and quite tall for his age, taller than his brother Jem, that's for sure. Today he's wearin' a pair of blue overalls and lace-up boots with no laces. And Billy . . .' he continued, warming to the subject, 'Billy's the baby of the family. He's got fair hair and blue eyes and all his clothes are ten sizes too big for him cos they're hand-me-downs. Them brown trousers he's wearin' with the holes in the knees belonged to my son Luke before he grew out of them,' concluded Uncle Jack, confident that he'd sorted the situation and the policeman would leave him alone.

The policeman was not to be dismissed that easily, however. A solemn-looking man, who clearly took his role as guardian of the peace very seriously, he rocked back and forth on his heels, considering Uncle Jack's statement.

'Well done, sir,' he said at length. 'You'd make an excellent witness in a court of law. You've given a very accurate description indeed of these two boys . . .' he paused . . . 'for a blind man.'

There was an excited murmur from the crowd and Uncle Jack's face turned from white to scarlet and back again in the space of two seconds. 'I . . . er . . .' he gulped. 'I know how they look cos they told me.'

'And they tell you every morning exactly what they're wearing, do they, sir?'

'Yeh . . . I mean, n-no,' stammered Uncle Jack, falling deeper and deeper into the trap. 'Cos they're always dressed the same.'

'Oh? And how do you know that, sir, in view of the fact that you can't see them?'

The crowd grew angry and began to shout.

'Cheat!'

'Scoundrel!'

'Liar!'

'Thief!'

'Chuck him in the chokey! Prison's the best place for the likes of him!'

'I think you'd better come along with me, sir,' said the policeman. 'But you can leave your white stick. You won't be needing that where you're going.'

'Oh crimes!' gasped Ned in dismay as the policeman snapped a pair of handcuffs on Uncle Jack and led him and his dog away. 'They'll put him in clink and it's all our fault.'

9

Clara was gagged, bound, blindfolded and thrown into the back of a cart. She heard a man cry, 'Get up, Daisy! Go on!' and the crack of a whip.

With a jolt the cart lurched forward, trundling over stones and sinking into ruts, throwing the girl from one side to the other. She could hear voices around her, happy voices, people laughing . . .

'Out of my way! Move over, there!' the man snarled as he drove the cart through the crowd.

Clara tugged at the ropes binding her hands and feet until she drew blood – but it was hopeless. She was trussed like a goose at the market. And her fate seemed as black as theirs. But though she was small, Clara was a fighter.

'I'll get away,' she said to herself with grim determination. 'I'll wait my moment, then I'll get away.'

10

The crowd chased Jem until he was hot and breathless, but gradually their hoarse shouts grew fainter until at last he had shaken them off. Stumbling behind one of the traders' caravans camped at the edge of Greenwich Park, Jem bent double to relieve the stitch in his side, still holding the bonnet and gloves Clara had given him. He knew it was foolish to keep them, but he could not bring himself to throw away anything, however dangerous, that he could sell for a few coins. And Clara's bonnet alone would fetch much more than that. It was a beauty, the very latest fashion – although Jem neither knew nor cared about that – an exquisite confection of satins and laces.

Jem had first met Clara when she was working the streets of London, sweeping dust and horse dung from the crossings in Trafalgar Square. And then, by a quirk of fate, she had been taken into the Strand Workhouse at the same time as him and his brothers. They had all escaped together, the three boys back to their caravan home in the Devil's Acre slum and Clara back to her mother and baby brother, Pip, in the dilapidated room in the heart of the Seven Dials rookery. And now Clara was in danger again. Worse danger. For while no one cared about the life or death of a poor girl, a rich one with a wealthy father was a different story.

In his mind's eye he saw her mother and father calling and calling her in vain until, when the terrible truth dawned on them, they went to the police, begging them to find her. Inevitably they would point the finger of suspicion at Jem. He was quite sure the police would be searching the fairground at that very moment for a short, stocky boy, about eleven years old, with a pug nose and eyes as black and full of mischief as a gremlin's. And as for his clothes, they were, to say the least, distinctive — a tailcoat, shiny with grease and age and so long it dragged on the ground, a threadbare waistcoat held together with pieces of string, a pair of one-legged trousers, spats, boots full of holes and a battered wideawake even dirtier than his hair. Jem had always prided himself on his dress, but for the first time he regretted his conspicuous finery. With so many policemen at the fair that day, he would be recognized and arrested the minute he stepped out of his hiding place, but somehow he had to get back to the freak show, he had to find Clara.

The door of the caravan opened abruptly and a girl came down the steps, staring at him.

'What're you doin' here?' she demanded, hands on hips.

'Admirin' the view,' retorted Jem, riled by her tone.

'Well, cut off and admire it somewhere else.'

'Goin' to make me, are you?'

'Nah, but my dad will when he comes home . . .' She frowned. 'What've you got behind your back?'

'Nothin',' said Jem.

'Don't believe you. You're hidin' somethin'.'

'Nah, I'm not . . .' Jem stopped as the germ of an idea took root in his brain. 'Oh all right, it's just a bonnet and gloves,' he said, showing them to her.

'Well, blow my wig!' she exclaimed, her eyes lighting up. 'I've never seen nothin' so splendacious. Where'd you get them? Nicked them off some rich kid, I'll wager.'

'I didn't. They belong to my sister.'

'Don't gammon me,' she laughed, casting a scornful eye over Jem's ragged clothes. 'No sister of yours ever wore a bonnet like that . . . Let me see.'

She snatched the bonnet from him and put it on.

'How do I look?' she said coyly.

It was on the tip of Jem's tongue to tell her the bonnet was several sizes too small and she looked ridiculous in it but that would have spoiled his plan, so, steeling himself to pay her a compliment, he muttered, 'You look jammy.'

'Oh Lor'!' she sighed, her face softening. 'If only I had a bonnet like, this I'd be the happiest girl alive.'

'You can have it,' said Jem.

'*What?*'

'I said you can have it.'

'Don't be soft, I haven't got the ready to buy it.'

'I'll swap you for it.'

'Swap what?'

'Them togs you're wearin'.'

'This old jacket and skirt?' She looked at him as if he'd taken leave of his senses.

'And your bonnet and boots. Everythin'.'

The girl did a quick calculation in her head. She could buy everything she stood up in for less than a shilling at any of the London markets, but the bonnet was worth — she took it off, running her fingers over the exquisite pink material — at least five shillings in one of the posh ladies' shops in Regent Street.

'All right,' she agreed, 'but I want the gloves as well.'

Without a murmur Jem handed them over. He was glad he'd kept Clara's silk scarf in his pocket or she would have wanted that too.

Scarcely believing her incredible luck, she ran into the caravan, took off her clothes, tied them in a bundle and put on her Sunday best, the only other outfit she possessed.

'There you are,' she said, handing her old clothes to Jem, her heart beating ten to the dozen for she feared he would surely come to his senses and realize what a terrible bargain he was making. But he took the bundle without a word, tucked it under his arm and walked away.

'I'll be jiggered,' laughed the girl, watching him go. 'I certainly got the better of him.'

11

The glorious spring sunshine had brought out the people of London by the thousand that Easter Monday and the fairground was full of men, women and children enjoying themselves – throwing sticks at pieces of gingerbread in the hope of winning one, riding the gaily decorated horses on the merry-go-rounds, flying high in the air on swings, watching a sailor dancing a hornpipe to the sounds of a cracked violin, eating pickled whelks – four big ones or six small for a penny. But their happy laughter and cheerful voices only mocked Ned's growing anxiety about Jem, and his face was white and tense in contrast to the relaxed, smiling faces around him.

'Where're we goin'?' panted Billy, struggling to follow his brother, who with his head lowered and his elbows out was hacking a path through the crowd.

'Lookin' for Ma,' said Ned.

'Why don't we go back to our pitch?'

'Cos she won't be there. Nobody'll be there. They're all out workin'. Come on, keep up, Lor's sake!'

'I can't, Ned,' whined Billy. 'I can't . . . run . . . no more.' And he crouched down to get his breath back.

Ned, unaware that his brother was no longer following him, ploughed on. Once or twice he thought he saw the familiar ragged shawl and tatty bonnet his mother wore, but when he shouted, 'Ma! Ma!' a strange face turned and looked at him blankly. By the time he realized that there was no little voice behind him bleating, 'Can't go on, Ned. Can't go on,' it was too late. Billy had gone.

In a panic Ned retraced his steps, crying, 'Billy! Billy!'

'Lor' bless you,' said a woman selling spiced nuts from a stall. 'It was "Ma, Ma" last time you passed, now it's "Billy, Billy." Sounds like you've lost everyone.'

Billy had run past the magsman doing the thimble-rigging dodge at least half a dozen times before it occurred to him that he was going round in circles. Though he shouted, 'Ned! Ned!' till he was hoarse, there was no answering cry, and when it finally dawned on him that he was utterly lost he sat down, put his head in his hands and cried.

People walked around him or tripped over him and some even ran their hands lightly over his body to see if he had anything worth stealing. Only one or two in that vast throng of revellers bent down to ask him what was wrong.

'My pa's in hospital and I've lost my ma and my brothers,' he sobbed.

'Dear me,' said a motherly woman with fourteen of her own children in tow, 'you'd best get yourself to a workhouse. They'll give you a bed and some grub.'

Billy had already been in a workhouse and he knew their beds were nothing but a pile of straw infested with fleas and lice and their food a bowl of hot water with a few wilted cabbage leaves floating in it. But since his attention span was not much longer than a gnat's he very soon forgot why he was crying, dried his eyes on the sleeve of his jacket, got up and wandered over to watch the thimble rigger at work. He was a weasel of a man, with flying fingers and eyes that darted here and there, never settling on anything or anyone for more than a second.

'Three thimbles and one pea, now you see them,

82

now you don't,' he sang out to the crowd standing around his table watching him eagerly. 'Three thimbles! Three thimbles! Movin' as quick as Jerry-go-Nimble,' he cried. And the crowd burst into laughter, for Jerry-go-Nimble was a common name for diarrhoea.

'I'll bet any gen'leman or lady a sovereign they can't say which thimble the pea is under,' said the man, moving the thimbles so fast that Billy, who had pushed his way to the front, felt quite dizzy watching them.

'I'll take any bet up to a crown . . . No, since it's Easter and I want to give you all a chance to enjoy yourselves, I'll take up to a sovereign. I can't say fairer than that, can I, ladies and gen'lemen?' he said, smiling innocently. 'I'm givin' money away today.'

The flying thimbles came to rest and the magsman waited for his first victim.

'I fancy it's under the third thimble,' said an affluent-looking man at the front of the crowd.

'I think you're right, Wally,' his wife agreed.

'No doubt about it, sir,' said a man standing on the other side of him. And lowering his voice he murmured, 'I saw it with my own eyes. It's under the third thimble right enough or my name isn't

John Smith. I only wish I had a sovereign to bet with.' And he sighed and shook his head.

Given such enthusiastic encouragement, the first man stepped forward and announced that he was putting a sovereign on the third thimble. And drawing the coin from his wallet and putting it on the table he looked round with a 'What a clever fellow am I' expression on his face.

'A sovereign I am bet. One sovereign I am bet on the third thimble, ladies and gents. Is the pea under that thimble? Is it or isn't it?' cried the magsman, prolonging the man's agony while the crowd roared, 'Lift it up! Lift it up!'

'Is it under there or not? Is it under . . . ?'

'Let's see! Lift it up!'

'Is it or isn't it? Is it or . . . ?' The magsman lifted the thimble with a flourish.

The people at the front of the crowd edged closer and those at the back stood on tiptoe and shouted, 'What happened? Was it there? Did he win?'

''Fraid not,' said the magsman sorrowfully, putting the sovereign into a money pouch slung at his side. 'Bad luck, guv.'

The crowd groaned in disappointment and people began to move away.

'Strange,' muttered the man who had just lost

his bet. 'I could have sworn I saw him put that pea under the third thimble.'

'Nah, he didn't. It isn't under none of them, mister,' piped up Billy in his piercing little voice. 'It isn't a pea neither. It's a bit of soft bread he can stick under his thumbnail. I know cos my uncle Percy does this dodge at the fair in Clapham. He makes a lot of money out of mugs like you,' he said, smiling sweetly at the man.

The crowd went silent, so astounded by the man's deception they could hardly believe their ears. The magsman gasped as if he had just received a sharp kick in the stomach, but he quickly regained control of himself and shouted, 'Don't listen to his giffle-gaffle, ladies and gents. Course the pea wasn't under the third thimble, cos it's under this one . . .'

But before he could pull another sly move to get himself out of a dangerous situation an athletic fellow leaped forward, grabbed the remaining two thimbles and lifting them up cried, 'The kid's right. There's nothing under any of them. The pea's under this varmint's thumbnail. Look!' And grabbing the magsman's hand he held it up for the crowd to see.

'Cheat!' protested the man who had lost the sovereign. 'Give me back my money, you scoundrel, or I'll have the law on you.'

'Cheat!' echoed the crowd, closing in on the magsman, who looked round wildly for a way of escape. But they were packed too closely around him now and he was trapped. Fearing a long stay in prison more than the loss of some of his money, he reached into the pouch, drew out a handful of coins, including the sovereign, and hurled them at the man, crying, 'There you are, guv. Now we're even.'

But the angry mob would have none of it.

'You're a dirty swindler!' they yelled.

'Rotten thief!'

'Liar!'

And they began to pummel him, pulling at his hair and clothes.

The magsman threw his money pouch to the man who'd called himself John Smith and shouted, 'Scarper, Gerry!' but before his partner in crime could run away a dozen men leaped on him too and, wrenching the pouch out of his grasp, tipped its contents on to the ground.

A mass of coins tumbled out – pennies, three-penny bits, sixpences, shillings, half-crowns, crowns, sovereigns – and men, women and children rushed to pick them up, screaming and cursing and elbowing each other out of the way in their greed.

Suddenly a cry went up: 'Crushers!'

Turning in alarm, they saw three or four burly constables bearing down on them, springing their rattles furiously and waving their truncheons.

The mob fled. And so did Billy. No matter that he was not involved in the magsman's dirty tricks, no matter that he hadn't managed to pick up any of the magsman's money because bigger, stronger hands had grabbed it all – when a Perkinski saw a policeman he automatically took to his heels.

12

The cart Clara was bouncing about in came to an abrupt halt and the driver hissed, 'Open this gate. Open it now, damn you!'

There came the sound of running feet and a bolt being drawn back. 'Sorry, guv. Sorry.' A grovelling voice. 'Didn't hear you.'

The cart rumbled downhill, the brakes screeching, until again it stopped.

Clara heard low voices, two men whispering, one with a heavy accent. She caught snatches of their conversation . . .

'I want money now, Slithe.'

'You'll have it when you've done your job, Paco.'

'But if police come, if police try arrest me . . .'

'They won't. We're too clever for them.'

'But if her papa don't give us money I no wait, I go back to Spain, I—'

'Don't worry, he'll give whatever we ask. He's sappy about the kid.'

'And my share, Slithe . . .?'

'One hundred, Paco, like we agreed.'

The foreigner had a harsh voice but the Englishman spoke softly, hissing the words menacingly. If a snake could speak, Clara thought, it would sound just like him. And the thought sent fear shimmering up and down her spine.

13

The jacket was too tight, the skirt too short, the lace-up boots pinched his toes and the bonnet kept tipping over his eyes but all in all, thought Jem, catching sight of himself in a pane of glass, he did look tolerably like a girl. He had to keep reminding himself not to stride along or kick everything in his path, like stones and bottles, because that wasn't the kind of thing girls did. And his voice . . . That was a dead giveaway. He had to make it high and squeaky or people would get suspicious.

Many times on his way back to the freak show he met policemen who were clearly searching for him, ducking in and out of tents and stopping to question any boy who fitted Jem's description, however remotely. But though his heart pounded like a big bass drum and his feet itched to run away Jem forced himself to mince along, taking small steps and looking demurely at the ground.

Once or twice a policeman stared at him rather

too keenly, as if he couldn't quite believe a girl would have such a face, with her nose bloodied and her eye blackened, but Jem smiled sweetly and said, 'Mornin', Your Honour,' and the policeman walked on, shaking his head pityingly.

When he got close to the freak-show tent he saw a trough from which several horses were drinking. Pushing one of them aside, Jem dunked Clara's scarf in the dirty water until it was well soaked. The ticket seller was sitting behind her table again, counting a large pile of coins, when he ran up, crying as if his heart would break.

'What's up, my ducky?' said the woman.

'It's my mum,' bleated Jem, dabbing at his cheeks with the wet scarf. 'I've lost my mum.'

'Ah, you poor thing,' said the woman sympathetically. 'When did you last see her?'

'Over there.' Jem pointed vaguely. 'I've looked everywhere. I've been in all the booths but . . .' His lower lip trembled. 'But she's gone. I can't find her.'

Jem squeezed the scarf so that more water flowed down his cheeks like tears.

'Don't take on so, my tulip,' said the woman. 'You'll find her sooner or later. Stands to reason. She wouldn't leave the fair without a sweet little thing like you, would she?'

'Could I look in there, missus?' Jem nodded at the entrance to the freak show. 'I haven't got the ready to buy no ticket but if I could go in just for a minute . . .' he finished with a sob.

The woman looked doubtful. She frowned and pursed her lips and drummed her fingers on the table in an agony of indecision. But as Jem turned away, his shoulders heaving, she called out, 'Oh, all right. But just for a minute, mind. I'll get into trouble if my guv'nor finds out I've let you in for nothin'. A boy, a right little varmint, cheated me into lettin' him in this mornin'. But I won't get caught like that twice, I can tell you. Nah, not me. And if I ever see that rascal again . . .' She shook her fist. Then her voice softened. 'Well, off you go then, plaguy quick, my pet,' she said. And went back to counting her money.

The tent was full of people, gazing in horror at the Prehistoric Man as he ripped the raw flesh off another gigantic bone, gasping in admiration as the Strong Man picked up a sack of bricks with his teeth, giggling at the Bearded Lady, who seemed to have grown an amazing amount of thick, black hair on her chest since Jem last saw her. But he was only interested in the Pirate and he barged through the crowd, enraging several people who snapped, 'Here, enough of that. You watch what you're doing with your elbows, miss.'

But when he got to the front Jem's mouth fell open, for the Pirate and his parrot had gone and in their place was a mermaid, her skin sea-green, her silvery hair covering her shoulders in wispy fronds. She lay on a rock, flapping her finny tail lethargically and gazing into space in a fishy kind of way.

'Oy!' Jem cried. 'Where's the Pirate?'

'Pirate?' The Mermaid opened and closed her mouth three or four times and stared at him with blank, grey eyes. 'What pirate?'

'The one that was here, with a parrot, with a wooden leg and a hook on his arm.'

'Funny kind of parrot,' said the Mermaid, to gales of laughter from the crowd.

'But he was here. He was,' insisted Jem. 'You're tellin' whoppers.'

At this the Mermaid became quite irate. 'I'm tellin' you there has never—' she shook her head so forcefully she nearly dislodged her long, silver wig — 'never been no pirate. So cut away, you pesky brat, before I set the Strong Man on you.'

'I'm not goin' till you tell me where the Pirate is,' said Jem. But in his rage he quite forgot he was supposed to be a girl and his voice came out as a hoarse shout.

'Here, you're a queer one and no mistake,' said a woman standing next to him. 'You look like a girl but you sound like a boy.'

'That's right, she does,' muttered someone else. 'What's her game, eh?'

'I've got a funny voice cos I . . . cos I've got two lots of tonsils,' said Jem, rather pleased with himself for having come up with such a neat solution.

'Two lots of tonsils?' exclaimed the woman. 'Lawks a mercy, my girl, sounds as if you should be in the freak show yourself.'

'I'd pay good money to see them,' said a man, drawing some coins from his pocket.

'Yeh, come on, open your mouth. Let's have a look,' said another.

But Jem had gone.

14

Clara was hauled out of the cart and thrown over someone's shoulder like a sack of coal. Galvanized into action, she twisted and writhed, kicking whoever was carrying her in the groin. He swore and flung her down so hard that she grunted with pain.

'¡*Cuidado!* Take care!' said the foreign man. 'You break her neck, we get nothing for her.'

The floor beneath Clara began to rock, then came the sound of lapping water and the swish, swish of oars as they rose and fell. Clara had seen many boats plying up and down the Thames, but she had never been on one. Was this a fishing boat or one of the watermen's or . . . her heart lurched – was it a pirate's? Her uncle Bob had told her what happened to children who were kidnapped by pirates and held to ransom . . . 'Merciless devils, they are. If the ransom isn't paid they think nothing of chuckin' the kids in the drink.' Clara's mind raced – where was the man taking her, out to sea, into that huge ocean Uncle Bob had told her about, vast, grey, full of monstrous creatures?

After what seemed an eternity the oars stopped dipping and rising and she felt the boat scrape alongside something and stop.

'*Bueno. You've got her,*' said a woman in Spanish. '*Dios mío, she's heavy for a little one,*' she grunted, as she hauled Clara aboard a three-masted fruit schooner with the name *La Gaviota* painted in gold letters on the side.

'*He feeds her well,*' muttered the man. '*Makes her fat.*'

'*He must be rich.*'

'*He's got enough to make us all rich.*'

'*I'll put her in the chain locker.*'

'*Muy bien. Nobody'll ever find her there — not till they pay up.*'

'*And if they don't . . .*'

'*We'll feed her to the fishes.*'

'*And that'll make them fat,*' cackled the woman.

It was as well Clara didn't understand Spanish.

15

The Greenwich police station on Blackheath Road was a busy place at any time of year but doubly so during the fair, when dozens of petty criminals from every corner of the country were crammed into the cells. The officer in charge was a Superintendent Blake and it was into his office that Clara's mother and father and Septimus Mallick were ushered when they reported Clara's abduction.

'It is my fault, I am entirely to blame,' said Mr Sterling over and over again. 'I warned Clara's governess that there are evil people who will stop at nothing to harm small children. I instructed her to watch over the girl at all times. And she did. She never let Clara out of her sight.'

'And where is the governess now, sir?' said Blake.

'She is unwell. She was most insistent that she should accompany us today, but in view of her indisposition my wife and I persuaded her to keep to her bed. In any case, it was unnecessary for her to come since we could take care of Clara … at least –' the poor man shook his head despairingly – 'we should have.'

'My dear sir, do not reproach yourself,' said Septimus Mallick in a vain attempt to comfort him. 'It is impossible to keep one's eye upon children every minute of the day.'

'Indeed it is,' agreed Superintendent Blake, who had sixteen of his own.

'But I have no doubt our excellent policemen will find Clara,' said Mallick, nodding approvingly at Blake.

'We'll do our best, sir,' said the superintendent, a heavy-set, ponderous man for whom Greenwich fair was the highlight of his year, if not his life. 'We are rather stretched at the present time on account of the vast influx of people descending upon us, but we shall do all we can to find the girl. Now then, Mr Sterling,' Blake perused the report the duty sergeant had written, 'are you quite sure the little girl didn't wander off, maybe to look at another booth?'

'No, no, superintendent. The last time we saw her she was talking with a boy . . . What was his name, my dear?' He turned to his wife.

'Jem Perkinski.'

'She was talking with this Jem Perkinski when

Mrs Sterling and I left the booth with Mr Mallick, my partner, to go to lunch.'

'And she did not follow you?'

'I had called her, superintendent, and was under the mistaken impression that she was following us.'

'So Clara remained in the booth?'

Mr Sterling nodded.

'With Jem Perkinski?'

'Indeed. And when we came back but moments later she had gone.'

'But that wretched boy had her bonnet and gloves and her neckerchief, a beautiful silk neckerchief Mr Sterling gave her for her birthday,' said Mrs Sterling, beginning to cry.

The superintendent looked grave and was about to say something when Mallick interrupted him. 'I fear this is the work of a professional gang,' he said. 'This Perkinski boy was probably used as a decoy.'

'A decoy, sir?' Mr Sterling frowned.

'I think Mr Mallick is suggesting that the boy deliberately kept the girl talking while everybody was lured outside by a fabricated story about an injured tightrope walker, thereby allowing a person or persons unknown to kidnap her,' said Blake.

'And do you believe Jem Perkinski is an accomplice, superintendent?' said Mr Sterling.

'I think it is highly likely, sir. He comes from a family well known to the police for their criminal activities. They attend the fair every year with the sole purpose of cheating and stealing. But kidnapping . . . I am surprised they have attempted something as despicable as that. Then again –' he sighed – 'maybe there is no limit to what the Perkinskis will get up to for money.'

'But you will surely apprehend them, sir?' said Mallick.

'Most definitely. We shall bring them all in for questioning.' Blake stopped and looked at Mallick thoughtfully. 'Perhaps you would be good enough to explain what brought you to the freak show, sir. It is surely not the kind of entertainment, if I may use the word,' he pursed his lips, 'in which, ahem, two gentlemen such as yourselves usually find themselves.'

'Indeed it is not, sir,' said Mr Mallick, looking abashed. 'But when my partner, Mr Sterling, told me that his daughter was enamoured of pirates, I recalled that I had heard say there was a splendid pirate in the freak show and recommended he take her. And it being a bright and sunny day I thought I too would go to the fair and, if I were fortunate enough to meet Mr Sterling and his family, invite them to take lunch with me. Had I known that Clara would be in any kind of danger . . .' he sighed, his voice trailing away.

'My dear Septimus, you are in no way to blame,' said Mr Sterling. 'How could you possibly have foretold such a misfortune?'

'Well, Mr Sterling,' Superintendent Blake leaned on the desk to lever himself upright, 'I suggest you return to your home and any developments will be reported to you as and when they occur.'

'Nah!' came an anguished cry from Clara's mother. 'I'm not leavin' till I've found my little girl.' And she ran out, brushing aside her husband's restraining hand.

'With your permission, sir, I too shall look for her,' said Mallick.

'That is very considerate of you, Septimus,' said Mr Sterling.

'In view of the kindnesses you have shown me over the many years of our partnership it is the very least I can do,' said Mallick. 'I only hope and pray it is not too late.'

16

By late afternoon the fairground was seething with revellers. To add to the din the crowd was making the vendors were also shouting their wares – pea soup, hot chestnuts, spiced nuts, gingerbread, fruit, milk – but above it all Jem made out a familiar voice. He stopped, straining to hear which direction it was coming from . . . Yes, over there, between the stilt-walkers and the fire-eaters, the shrill tone was unmistakable.

'All the way from Egypt, ladies'n gen'lemen,' Gran was crying. 'The Miracle of Life is brought to you all the way from Egypt by gallopin' camels.'

'What's it made of?' asked the man who had appointed himself the old lady's official tormentor for the day.

'Asses' milk.'

'Asses' milk? Lor', why'd you have to bring it here from Egypt? We've got plenty of asses in this coun-try. Matter of fact,' he cast a withering look at some of the oafish faces around him, 'we've got quite a few here today. I reckon you could milk them for all they've got.'

'This is special milk from special asses,' said Gran, turning her back on him. 'It's what Cleopatra used in her bath.'

'Must be pretty dirty then.'

'Who's Cleopatra?' asked a woman.

'She was the Queen of Egypt, the most beautiful woman in the world. And you will be too, ladies, if you use my Miracle of Life. Just one drop . . .' Gran held up the bottle, 'just one little drop will take away all your wrinkles and warts and make you look like a young girl again.'

'Do you use it?' asked the wag.

'Course I do,' said Gran stoutly.

'So why do you look like a prune's grand-mother?'

'Cos I've just started using it. But she's been usin' it for years.' Gran pointed at her granddaughter, who was ogling a boy. 'And how old d'you think she is?'

The wag looked intently at Kate's freckled face and bright red hair. 'About fourteen, I reckon.'

Kate was about to say he was dead right, she had

turned fourteen in March, when Gran cut in. 'She's older than me.'

'*What?*' The crowd gasped.

'Well, stands to reason, doesn't it, seein' as how she's my great-grandmother.'

'*Your great . . .?* Blimey!' exclaimed a woman. 'Give me a bottle, plaguy quick!'

Immediately a forest of hands reached out, eagerly offering a coin in return for the magical potion they believed would restore their lost youth.

Jem pushed his way through the crowd and tugged at the old lady's arm. 'Gran,' he hissed in her ear. 'Gran, I need your help. I need it real bad.'

She glanced at him and frowned. 'I'm sorry, my ducky,' she said. 'Even the Miracle of Life couldn't do nothin' for a mug like yours.'

'But, Gran . . .'

'And stop callin' me gran.'

'But you are my gran.'

'Now hook it, my girl, or I'll . . .!'

'Gran,' the boy lowered his voice, 'I'm Jem.'

'Jem?' she screeched.

'Shh! Hold your jaw, Lor's sake,' pleaded Jem, looking around nervously.

'Why're you dressed like that?' demanded the old woman.

'I had to disguise myself cos the crushers are after me.'

'What've you been up to?'

'I gulled sixpence out of a bloke with them cigars Ma makes and I gulled a woman to let me and Ned and Billy into the freak show for nothin' and then I got a bonnet and gloves and neckerchief off a girl.'

'Sounds like a good mornin's work,' said Gran approvingly.

'Nah, it all went bad after that, real bad.'

'You'd best tell me where no one can hear,' said Gran, seeing his anxious face. 'Kate,' she called to her granddaughter, 'look after the stall while I have a little chat with this . . . er . . . young lady. And, Kate, don't lose the money. And don't spend it neither. Now what's all this about?' she asked when she and Jem were well out of earshot of any eavesdroppers.

'We were in the freak show, Gran, and everybody ran out to see a bloke who'd broke both his legs, only he hadn't, and I got clobbered and just as I was gettin' up I saw somebody nab a kid, a girl, and drag her away.'

'Sounds like a nasty business,' said Gran. 'But kids disappear all the time and nobody never knows what's happened to them. They're gone and that's the end of it. There's nothin' you nor me can do about . . .'

'But they're blamin' me, Gran, cos I was the only one left in the tent, and when everybody came back they saw me with her bonnet and stuff.'

'You nicked them?'

'Nah, she gave them to me. She did!' Jem insisted, as Gran narrowed her eyes. 'And then they all started screamin' and chasin' me.'

'But they don't know who you are, son. So long as you keep your head down, you'll be safe.'

'But they do know who I am, Gran, cos Clara, that's the girl, was in the Strand Workhouse with me and Ned and Billy. She knows my name and where I live. So does her mum.'

'Lor' bless you. You're in real trouble and no flies,' agreed Gran. 'You'd best get out of here plaguy quick, son. Go back to Devil's Acre.'

'Nah, that's no use, the crushers'll catch me. They're probably there right now lookin' for me. I've got to find Clara, Gran. I've got to find her, cos she's the only one that can tell the crushers I didn't have nothin' to do with it.'

'But where're you goin' to find her, you ninny?' snapped Gran. 'If someone's kidnapped her, how're you goin' to find out who did it and where she is?'

'It happened at the Pirate's booth,' said Jem. 'But when I went back to the freak show to see him he'd gone and there was a mermaid in his booth, only she said there'd never been no pirate there. But she's lyin', Gran. I'll wager she knows what happened to Clara.'

'Mm, sounds like there's somethin' fishy goin' on.'

'But she won't tell me what it is, Gran. She won't.'

'There, there, my ducky,' said the old lady. 'No one's goin' to put you in clink if I can help it. Let's go and see that pesky Mermaid. I'll soon make her talk.'

17

Clara had lost all sense of time. How long had she been trapped in the dark, she wondered, doubled up, scarcely able to move, the ropes biting into her wrists and ankles, the gag making her mouth sore? She had never been in a boat before and the strange noises disturbed her, the constant creaking and groaning, as if it too were in pain. And the motion – the way *La Gaviota* rose and fell with every wave, pitching and tossing until her stomach protested and she felt the gorge rise in her throat.

At length she heard footsteps above her, the sound of a hatch being lifted and then her blindfold was untied and pulled away. A hatchet-faced woman with iron-grey hair pulled back in a bun stared down at her.

Clara, blinking in the sunlight, looked around her. She was in a cabin . . . no, not a cabin, a cubby-hole, a space so small the ceiling was barely a foot above her head and the walls so close she could have reached out to touch them.

'So, *niña*,' said the woman, and her voice was as steely as her face, 'I take this off.' She tugged at the knot of Clara's gag. 'No scream,' she said. 'Is a waste of time. Everyone scream here. You listen . . .' She put her hands over her ears in a mocking gesture, for the noise from the hundreds of boats on the river was truly deafening, with men shouting, laughing, arguing and barking commands.

With another tug the woman pulled the gag free.

'Ah, no scream,' she scoffed, as Clara glared at her balefully, keeping her mouth tightly shut. '*Bueno*. Is good. Now I bring you to eat,' she said. 'But I leave your hands and feet . . . er . . . how you say? Tied. I leave tied or you run away, no?' She gave a nasty laugh, revealing big, square teeth like gravestones. 'But you not go till your papa give us –' she made a rubbing motion with her thumb and forefinger – 'lot of money.'

And, still cackling, she put down the hatch and went away.

18

As the afternoon wore on, lights sprang up all over the fairground, candles and smoky flares illuminating the hundreds of stalls and sideshows. It seemed to Ned there were more people than ever, some of them already quite drunk on port and sugar or hot gin and peppermint. The hot-chestnut man was doing a brisk trade and the fish stalls had set out enticing little dishes of pickled salmon, jellied eels, cockles, whelks and oysters.

Ned saw his sister Kate in the Crown and Anchor, a large marquee set up for the duration of the fair with a boarded floor for dancing. She was chatting and laughing, while all around her men with cigars jammed between their lips were whirling their partners around with such enthusiasm they bumped into other couples and sent them flying until everyone on the dance floor ended up in a heap.

'Kate!' cried Ned, hammering on the window and waving frantically to get her attention. 'Kate!'

The door flew open and a very irate woman came out. 'You bang that window any harder, my lad, and you'll smash it,' she scolded him. 'Then you'll have to cough up the ready to have it repaired.'

'But I've got to see my sister, missus. It's real important.'

'Have you got sixpence to get in?'

'Nah, I haven't got nothin'.'

'Then you'll have to wait till she comes out, won't you?'

'When'll that be?'

'How the devil do I know?'

'But I've got to see her now. If you just let me in for a minute . . .'

'Oh yeh.' The woman put her hands on her hips and gave a nasty laugh. 'I know your sort – "Just let me in for a minute for free . . ." I wish I'd had a hot dinner for the number of times I've heard that one. Well, you can't come in here unless you've got the ready, you toerag. And if you haven't, then hook it!' She finished with a jerk of the thumb.

'But . . .'

'Hook it, I said. If you're not gone by the time I

count three, I'll call a crusher. And you too,' she shouted at a small boy who was standing at the window, his nose pressed against the glass, staring at a table inside on which were displayed plates of beef, tongue, ham, chicken, rolls and butter. 'Pack off, the pair of you.'

And she went back in, slamming the door behind her.

'Billy?' said Ned, as the other boy turned towards him.

'Ned?'

'Where've you been?'

'Lookin' for you,' cried Billy, running to his brother and wrapping himself around his knees.

'And I've been wastin' time lookin' for you. Come on,' said Ned, grabbing his arm. 'Let's find Ma.'

'But I'm hungry, Ned. My belly's murderin' me. I haven't had nothin' to eat for so long I've forgotten how to swallow.'

'We've got to keep goin',' insisted Ned, trying to pull the little boy along.

'Nah,' cried Billy, falling on his face and hammering the ground with his fists and feet. 'Won't go! Won't!'

Grabbing him by the scruff of the neck, Ned

dragged Billy along, muttering what he was going to do to the little boy if he didn't walk properly, but Billy prised himself free of his brother's grasp and ran up to a stall selling pies and patties and cut meats. 'Cor, look,' he cried. 'Wish I could have some of that.' And he fixed his eyes on a pork pie with such a hypnotic stare that it was surprising the pie didn't leap off the plate and slide down his throat.

There were many people milling around the stall and the owner and his wife were briskly answering requests for 'a dish of pigs' trotters, guv' or 'a slice or two of ox tongue, missus,' or 'a nice bit of blood puddin'.

Ned was as hungry as Billy, but without Jem's quick wit to help them and with nothing to sell or trade there was little they could do but beg – and there were far too many beggars at the fair, all accosting people with outstretched hands and pleading eyes. Ned ran his eyes over the tempting display, his mouth watering so much he started to dribble.

'Come on, Billy,' Ned said, 'it's only makin' it ten times worse, lookin' at all that grub.' But as he turned away a woman in a flounced skirt, bonnet and lace shawl passed by with two little girls in tow.

'Oh, Mama,' said one, 'please buy me one of

those scrumptious little pigeon pies. You know how I adore them.'

'Why, Emily, you cannot possibly be hungry,' laughed the woman.

'Oh, please, Mama,' cried the other girl, tugging at her mother's arm, 'I should like one too.'

'Very well, my sweet.'

The woman reached into a pocket in the front of her skirt and drew out a purse from which she took a sixpenny piece. Replacing the purse, she held up the coin in her gloved hand to attract the attention of the stallholder and his wife.

Ned watched the woman like a hungry cat watching a particularly juicy mouse, but the boy was in a quandary and he looked anxiously about him, gnawing his fingernails. If he was caught picking pockets or stealing, the punishment was several years' hard labour in one of London's prisons, or, if the magistrate was very severe, he could be deported to Australia. And Australia was a harsh land where many a strong, healthy boy died, grieving for his home and family.

Billy slumped dejectedly, staring at all the people swarming around him who were gorging themselves on kidney puddings and mutton patties.

Every so often he clutched his stomach and whimpered, 'Hungry. Hungry.'

Ned looked at the woman and her daughters in their fine clothes and then at his brother in his dirty rags, his little face white and pinched . . . 'Billy,' he hissed at him. 'Billy, come here.' And pulling him to one side Ned whispered in his ear, 'When I give you the word, run as hard as you can and knock one of them kids over. Then say you're sorry, you weren't lookin' where you were goin'.'

'Why?'

'Cos I know how we can get the ready to buy some grub.'

'But what if their ma gets angry? What if she tans my hide?'

'Look, do you want a pork pie or not?'

As soon as he heard the magic words, Billy needed no further persuasion. With head lowered like a charging bull and a fierce expression on his face he waited for Ned to give the signal before running full tilt at the smaller of the two girls, butting her in the back so hard that she fell forward against the stall with a cry of pain.

'Louise, my darling,' cried her mother. 'What on earth . . . ?'

'That stupid boy did it, Mama,' said the other girl, pointing at Billy.

'Sorry, missus,' said Billy, looking very pleased with himself. 'I wasn't lookin' where I was goin'.'

'You foolish child,' chided the woman, taking in Billy's dirty face and bare feet with a look of distaste. 'That was an unforgivable thing to do.'

'Sorry, missus,' Billy repeated. 'I wasn't lookin' where I was goin'.'

Ned was extremely nervous. He had never done a proper dodge without Jem, and there were many policemen at the fair that day on the lookout for pickpockets.

Billy, beginning to sound like a parrot, said, 'Sorry, missus. I wasn't lookin' where I was goin',' yet again, and the woman shooed him away with a wave of her hand. But he wouldn't budge. He had been promised a pork pie and he wasn't about to leave until he got it.

'Have you hurt yourself, my darling?' asked the woman, fussing over her daughter while the other girl put her arm around her sister's waist and gazed into her face with a concerned expression.

'I am all right, Mama.'

'You brave little angel. I knew it was unwise to

116

'come to this dreadful place,' said the woman, glancing balefully at Billy.

'They are all of the lower class,' said her daughter disdainfully, looking down her nose at the costermongers and kitchen maids milling around them.

'Indeed they are,' agreed her mother. 'We shall go home as soon as poor, dear Louise has quite recovered.'

While the woman was engaged with her daughters, Ned edged towards her until he was almost touching her. He crossed his arms and stared straight ahead, running one hand over her skirt until he found the pocket. Then, with a quick look to left and right to make sure nobody was watching, he pulled out the purse. Still using his arm as a cover, he slid the purse across his chest and was just about to hide it in the bib of his overalls when Billy, growing impatient, cried, 'Ned, I've said I'm sorry to that old biddy three times now. Haven't you got the ready yet?'

The woman turned sharply, saw Ned with her purse in his hand and cried, 'Thief! Thief!'

Ned froze. Then, recovering his senses, he grabbed Billy and ran like the wind.

There was a hubbub of angry voices and everywhere people seemed to be shouting, 'Thieves! Thieves! Stop those boys!'

Ned and Billy barged through the crowd, bowling people over, dodging around tents and stalls, under swings, round the marionettes and through the German band, sending the trombone player sprawling on his back. But still the crowd followed, baying loudly, like bloodthirsty huntsmen after two frightened little foxes.

19

Ma Perkinski was tired. She and Cousin Annie had trudged around the fairground for hours trying in vain to sell their tulips and daffodils. As the day wore on the flowers drooped and so did the two women. Finally they dumped the wilted blooms and took to begging.

It seemed that everybody had gone to the fair with their pockets full of coins, but they chose to spend them on the swings and merry-go-rounds and coconut shies and sideshows rather than put them into the outstretched hands of Ma and Cousin Annie.

The two women tried in vain to soften their hearts with pleas of, 'Spare a penny for a poor gypsy, guv,' and 'You've got a kind face, missus. Help a poor woman that's down on her luck.'

'Oh, I've had enough,' said Ma, sitting on the grass. 'We can't beg, borrow nor steal nothin', Annie. We might as well take the weight off our feet.' And she pulled off her boots with a sigh of relief.

'It's been a bad day all round, love,' agreed Cousin Annie, 'what with your Bert breakin' his ribs and poor old Jack copped for his blind-beggar dodge. I don't know what the world's comin' to, straight I don't. There's no justice in it for decent-livin' folk the likes of us.'

'I only hope Jem and Ned make a bit of money. If Jem sells the rest of them cigars and Ned sells some of the stuff on my tray we should have enough to buy some grub tonight. I could do with somethin' after all this trampin' around. I'm fair done up. And my dogs are barkin' somethin' awful,' Ma moaned, rubbing her aching feet.

'I'm sure your boys will've done well, Liza,' said Cousin Annie, sinking down beside her and loosening her stays. 'You can always rely on Jem to use his upper storey. He's a sharp lad.'

'But he only gets ha'pennies and pennies, Annie. We need more than that. Bert brings in a crown every week workin' at the market, but who's goin' to look after me and my boys while my old man's flat on his back in hospital enjoyin' himself?'

'Don't you worry, my tulip.' Cousin Annie

patted Ma's arm comfortingly. 'You've got a good family. We'll look after you.'

'Oh, thanks very much, love,' said Ma with feeling.

'You can work on Arthur's stall in the market during the day. He's in sore need of another pair of hands, what with his wife bein' taken queer again. Then you can help me with my washin' and ironin'. I've built up a crack trade, more than I can cope with alone. And you can give Sid a hand in his pub at night. The poor fellow's fair run off his feet, so I know he'd find plenty for you to do. And in your free time you could help his missus. With fifteen kids and another one on the way I know she'd appreciate it and she'd give you a penny or two.'

'Oh, that's real kind of you, Annie,' said Ma. 'Very kind indeed, I must say.'

'Think nothin' of it, Liza.'

'I don't think nothin' of it,' retorted Ma hotly. 'And if that's your idea of lookin' after me I'll look after myself, thanks. I'm not washin' and ironin' and scrubbin' and runnin' round after you lot day and night. A penny or two . . .? Huh!'

'Well, I never!' huffed Cousin Annie. 'There's gratitude for you. I do my best to help you out and all you can say is . . . Hey up! Somebody's in for it!'

 121

she said as shouts of 'Stop them! Stop those boys!' filled the air.

'They're probably after a couple of buzzers.' Ma shrugged. 'There are too many pickpockets at the fair, if you ask me. And most of them are green-horns. They deserve to be caught.' And she lay back on the grass with a sigh of relief and closed her eyes.

The next minute two boys went hurtling by, their faces wild with fear, followed closely by several dozen men and women, shaking their fists and yelling fit to wake a congregation.

'Lawks a mercy!' shrieked Cousin Annie. 'Them was your two, Liza. It was Ned and little Billy.'

'What?' Ma sat up. 'You sure, Annie?'

'Course I am. And they've got half the fair chasin' them from the looks of it. Here, wait for me, duck,' she said, as Ma pulled on her boots and got to her feet. 'I'm comin' with you.'

But since she was a very stout woman it took her several minutes to lever herself upright, by which time Ma had gone.

20

Away from the bustle and noise of the fairground was a park where families could sit on the grass, picnicking, the parents stretched out, enjoying a snooze in the warm sunshine, the children playing Kiss in the Ring and Thread My Grandmother's Needle.

Young clerks who spent the rest of the year working from dawn to dusk in some dreary office frolicked with their sweethearts, servant girls freed for one brief moment from the drudgery of sweeping, scrubbing and polishing fine houses.

Up the steep hill to the Greenwich Observatory they ran, only to tumble all the way down again, skirts flying, bonnets askew, the boys snatching kisses, the girls giggling, fending them off, or pretending to, with cries of, 'Stop it, Joe, do!'

Not one of them saw Slithe hiding in the bushes, his long, thin, sinuous body curled into a tight ball, or they would have stopped laughing and run for their lives. But he was alone, alone with his bottle of gin and his black thoughts. He slithered further into the undergrowth, cursing, always the same curses: for the midwife who had dragged him into the world hideously disfigured; for his mother who had cried out in horror when she saw him and left him to die; for the men, women and children who had tormented him throughout his childhood, calling him a monster, a fiend, a child of darkness, and chased him away with sticks and stones.

'To hell with them all,' he muttered, his thin lips curling in a contemptuous sneer.

As the shadows lengthened he sighed and coiled and uncoiled his serpentine body restlessly. He was waiting for nightfall, waiting impatiently for the mantle of darkness to protect him as he went about his evil business. Time and again he upended the gin bottle and poured its burning contents down his throat until it was empty and, swearing, he hurled it against a tree.

A rubber ball rolled into the bushes and touched his foot. He pushed it away, writhing as if he'd been stung.

'It went that way,' he heard a woman cry. 'Over there, Connie.'

'I can't find it, Mum.'

'Connie, not there. In the bushes, I said. Lor', child, haven't you got eyes in your head?'

The bushes parted and a young girl appeared. At the sight of the ball her face lit up.

'I've found it, Mum,' she shouted. But in stooping to pick it up she suddenly saw Slithe curled up at the foot of a tree staring at her. She opened her mouth to scream but he was on her, gripping her throat, his hands cold as ice.

'You be quiet, missy,' he hissed. 'You tell anyone you saw me here and I'll cut your tongue out.' He pulled a knife from his sleeve. 'D'you understand?' He shook her hard. 'Do you?'

The girl stared at him, too terrified to speak.

'All you got to say is yes. That's all.' He prized her mouth open and dug the tip of the knife lightly into her tongue. 'Well?'

The girl tried to say something but only a gurgling, choking sound came out.

'Again!' rasped Slithe, lifting the knife so that she could speak.

'I . . . I . . .'

'Say it!'

'Yes,' she whispered, so softly he could barely hear it.

'Good.' He thrust her away. 'Now take your ball and pack off.'

The girl half stumbled, half ran back to her mother.

'Why, Connie, you look all to pieces. What's wrong, my treasure?' said the woman.

Slithe listened intently, his tongue darting in and out, moistening his dry, cracked lips.

'N-nothing,' stammered the girl. 'Let's go home, Mum.'

'But I thought you wanted to stay and see the fireworks?'

'Mum, please . . .' The girl darted a nervous glance over her shoulders, 'let's go home.'

And taking her mother's hand, she pulled her away.

21

'Not so plaguy fast,' complained Gran, hobbling along behind Jem.

'Oh come on, Lor's sake. We're never goin' to get there at this rate. All the freaks'll have packed up and gone.'

'How much does it cost to get into their show?'

'Twopence. A penny for you and a penny for me.'

'A penny? That's daylight robbery.'

'You charge threepence for the muck you sell.'

'The Miracle of Life is not muck. It's a special potion made of ass's milk and—'

'Don't kid me, Gran. I've seen you make it,' said Jem scornfully. 'It's pig's fat and vinegar and crushed weeds, same as you put in all your stuff.'

'Ullo, my lovey. So you found your mum, I see,' said the woman sitting outside the freak show as Jem ran up.

'Nah, this is my gran. I'm still lookin' for my mum,' said Jem in a high voice.

'Well, you won't find her in the show cos there's no one in there,' said the woman. 'They've all been frightened away by the crushers.'

'Crushers?' echoed Jem and Gran in horrified unison.

'Swarmin' all over the place since a little kid was nabbed. Said they're lookin' for a boy, a wicked rascal by the sound of it, brown hair, black eyes, pointed ears . . . They said if I was to see one like him I was to tell them straight away.'

'Are the crushers still in there?' asked Jem nervously, dipping his head so that his bonnet slipped down to cover more of his face.

'Nah, they've gone. But they'll be back – more's the pity,' said the woman, looking downcast. 'Ruinin' our business, they are. Nobody wants to go nowhere near the place cos of what happened. I haven't sold half a dozen tickets all afternoon.'

'And I had my heart set on seein' them freaks,' said Gran wistfully. 'Tell you what, my ducky, I'll give you some of my Miracle of Life if you let me and my granddaughter in there for nothin',' she said, taking a bottle out of her pocket.

'Miracle of Life?' said the woman, looking doubt-

fully at its murky contents. 'What's it supposed to do?'

'Depends how much you take. One sip'll make you look like a young woman, two'll make you look like a girl and if you take three you'll end up a baby again in your ma's belly.'

'Well, I'll be jiggered,' exclaimed the woman. 'How long does it take to work?'

'About . . .' Gran did a quick calculation. She and Jem would need no longer than thirty minutes in the freak show, plus a few minutes to get well clear of the place before the ticket seller discovered that no matter how much Miracle of Life she drank she still looked like a tortoise . . . 'Less than an hour. But you'd best warn your family and friends before you take it, else they'll never recognize you.'

'Crikey, that old codger's right,' whispered Jem, following Gran into the tent. 'There's no one here. And no freaks neither,' he said, walking quickly past all the empty booths. 'Where've they gone?'

'Perhaps the crushers've copped them. Nah, listen, I think I can hear somethin'.'

Sure enough, as they drew closer to the Man Mountain's booth, Jem and Gran could hear sounds of chattering and laughter.

129

'They must be behind there,' said Gran, pointing to an ornate screen at the back of the booth. 'Come on, let's go and take a look.'

'Nah, Gran, I just thought of somethin',' said Jem, pulling her back. 'If the Mermaid's there, she'll recognize me.'

'What of it?'

'She'll get snappish if she sees me again. She won't talk.'

'Yeh, you're right.' Gran nodded. 'You'd best disguise yourself.'

'I have disguised myself – I'm dressed like a pesky girl, aren't I? Here, tell you what, let's swap bonnets,' said Jem. And taking his own off he put Gran's tatty one on his head, tying the strings under his chin. 'And give me your shawl,' he said, wrapping the raggedy garment around his shoulders. Then, crossing his eyes and sucking in his cheeks as if he was eating a lemon he said, 'There, how do I look?'

'Your own ma wouldn't recognize you,' said Gran, nodding approval. 'Now come on. And be careful. Mind that lot,' she said, indicating the piles of rough-edged paving stones and bricks and iron cannonballs the Man Mountain used in his act. But Jem couldn't resist picking up one of the cannonballs – just to see if he had the strength. Cupping his hands around it and gritting his teeth, he flexed his muscles and heaved . . . And fell over backwards. The cannonball flew out of his hands, bounced gently two or three times and rolled to the edge of the booth.

'Lawks a mercy,' said Gran, picking it up. 'It's made of rubber.'

'So's these bricks,' said Jem, tossing one in the air. 'The Man Mountain's a dirty cheat.'

'A common thief,' agreed Gran. 'Takin' our hard-earned money on false pretences. He should be locked up.'

'Let's see what he's doin',' said Jem. And he and Gran peered round the screen.

A group of men and women were sitting at a table eating hunks of grey bread liberally spread with thick, white dripping and drinking tankards of ale.

'They're not freaks,' scoffed Gran, 'they're frauds,' for the Bearded Lady had taken off her beard and moustache, the woman with two heads had unpinned one and hung it on a peg, the Prehistoric Man reached into the pocket of his lion's skin, pulled out a packet of cigarettes and said, 'Smoke, anyone?' before lighting one for himself, and the Mermaid had removed her tail and long, silver wig.

131

But even though she was still painted a sickly shade of green, Jem immediately recognized her.

'That woman,' he hissed in Gran's ear. 'She was the one who came runnin' in to say a bloke'd fallen off a tightrope. Only it wasn't true, Gran. I'll wager she did it to get everyone out of the tent so that whoever nabbed Clara could do it without bein' seen.'

'But she's supposed to be a mermaid. Mermaids can't run — well, not with a tail, they can't.'

'She wasn't pretendin' to be a mermaid then, Gran. There was no mermaid in the show, I'll swear to it. She's coverin' up for the Pirate.'

'Right, we'll soon find out what she's up to,' whispered Gran. But the Mermaid had heard her, for she leaped to her feet and cried, 'Do you mind? We're havin' our supper.'

'Yeh, pack off!' said the others, their faces reflecting a mixture of indignation and alarm.

'Now, now, my dearies, there's no need to upset yourselves,' said Gran in a sugary voice. 'I'm just doin' my job, same as you.'

'And what might that be?' said the Prehistoric Man, 'A pig's nark?'

'I'll wager she is,' said the Bearded Lady. 'Them pesky crushers've sent her to spy on us.'

132

'We've had enough of them askin' us questions all day long, accusin' us of kidnappin' that little girl.'

'Yeh, kick her out!'

They advanced on Gran with clenched fists, muttering and swearing at her and Jem in a very menacing fashion.

'I'm not a spy,' protested Gran. 'I'm a gypsy, a true Romany and I've come here to offer my help. I've got medicines that'll cure you of anythin' from colic to cholera. I've got charms that'll bring you luck in love. I've got potions that'll make you look years younger . . .' She gave Jem a warning look. 'I've got magic spells that'll destroy your enemies. I can tell your fortune . . .'

'How much?' asked the Mermaid eagerly. 'How much for tellin' me my future?'

'I'll do it for nothin' for you, my pet, cos I like the look of you' said Gran slyly.

'Nah, me first,' said the Bearded Lady, pushing the Mermaid roughly aside and thrusting her hand at Gran.

Gran took it in hers and studied the woman's palm for a moment or two. 'You've had a hard life, my poppet,' she said.

'You can say that again,' said the Bearded Lady with feeling. 'What with my old man . . .'

'Takin' off sudden like that,' said Gran with a knowing nod.

The woman frowned. 'He didn't take off; he died.'

'Takin' off for heaven is what I meant.'

'Heaven? That old devil? Hell, more like. Leavin' me . . .'

'With all them kids.'

'What kids? I never had none.'

'But you will,' said Gran. 'I can see them in your hand, six of them.'

'Get off, I'm too old to have kids.'

'Oh come on, Ethel, it's my turn,' said the Mermaid impatiently, pushing her hand under Gran's nose.

'Here, she hasn't finished with me yet, Ruby. I want to know who the father of them six kids is, seein' as how I haven't got a husband.'

'Nah, and not likely to get one neither.'

'Oh, and why not . . . ?'

'Now then, enough caterwaulin', you two,' said Gran. And grabbing the Mermaid's hand she looked at it closely and muttered, 'Oh dear! Oh dear! This is real bad, Ruby.'

The woman swallowed hard. 'Why? What's wrong? What can you see?'

'Trouble. Danger,' said Gran grimly. 'But it's not clear — not to me anyhow. My pretty little grand-daughter here will tell you though. She's got the gift.'

'What gift?'

'She can see things, things that have happened, things that will happen.'

'What, with cross eyes?'

'She can see all right, better than you and me,' insisted Gran, 'though she does uncross her eyes when she goes into a trance,' she added, giving Jem a nudge with her knee to remind him.

'What's a trance?' said Ruby.

'It's when you seem to be asleep, only you're not,' said Gran.

'Sounds like a load of giffle-gaffle to me,' growled the Prehistoric Man. 'I wouldn't have nothin' to do with it, if I was you, Ruby.'

'Nah!' Ruby cut him short with a nervous gesture. 'I want to know. I must know. What danger?' She grabbed Gran's arm, digging her fingers in so hard the old woman flinched. 'What will happen to me? Tell me! Tell me!'

'Are you willin' to go into a trance to help this poor woman, Jemima?' Gran said to Jem.

'Yeth, I am, Granny,' said Jem, who had decided a lisp would help his disguise.

'And you know what you've got to do, don't you, my ducky?' she said, giving Jem a surreptitious wink.

'Yeth, Granny.'

'Right.' The old lady reached into the top of her sequined jacket and drew out the bottom of a broken beer bottle on a string.

'What's that?' said Ruby.

'It's a magic crystal. A witch gave it me.'

Ruby shuddered. 'And what's it supposed to do?'

'It makes Jemima feel sleepy. She keeps watchin' it till she goes into a trance,' Gran explained, swinging the bit of glass back and forth, back and forth in front of Jem's face.

Out of the corner of his eye Jem could see the others looking at him intently, but none as intently as Ruby. She sat clenching and unclenching her fists and running her tongue over dry lips.

Jem felt a sneeze coming on, but he did his best to stop it by squeezing his lips together and twitching his nose.

'Why's she doin' that?' asked Ruby.

'To let me know she's gone into a trance,' explained Gran. 'Now, Jemima,' she leaned towards him, 'tell me what you see, my tulip. All of it, mind.'

Jem fluttered his eyelids and began swaying from side to side. He was quite pleased with this because it looked spooky, he thought – but not spooky enough, so he opened his mouth wide, threw back his head and let out a series of blood-curdling yelps of the kind a soul in torment might make. He was warming to this performance, adding to it a violent shaking of his hands and feet when Gran growled, 'Get on with it, Jemima.'

'Oh, right,' said Jem. 'Well, it'th like thith, Gran. I can thee a little kid, a girl. She'th about thith high . . .' He held out his hand. 'And she'th wearin' a jammy dreth and booth . . .'

'What the devil's she sayin'?' snapped Ruby. 'I can't understand a word. Does she have to lisp so much?'

'It's cos her mouth's a bit funny,' explained Gran. 'You see, it's cos she's got . . .'

For one terrible moment Jem thought Gran was going to say he'd got two lots of tonsils . . . 'A fat tongue,' he said quickly.

'Yeh, that's right,' the old lady nodded. 'But try to speak proper, Jemima, do,' she added, giving him a warning look, 'so this lady can understand you.'

'Thorry . . . I mean, sorry, Gran. I said I can see a little kid, a girl. And she's wearin' a jammy dress and

137

boots and a pink bonnet and . . . Nah, wait a minute, she's takin' off her bonnet and gloves and givin' them to a boy standin' next to her, a good-lookin' boy, sharp as they come, a smart dresser too. He's wearin'—'

'Never mind about him, Jemima,' Gran snapped. 'Tell us what's happenin' to the girl.'

'Well, Gran, she's lookin' at a pirate and his parrot . . .'

There was a sharp intake of breath from Ruby.

'But now a woman's come runnin' in, shoutin' somethin' about a bloke fallin' off a tightrope — only, if you ask me it's a load of rubbish. There never was no bloke . . .'

'Just tell us what you see, Jemima,' Gran warned him.

'Oh . . . Oh right, Gran. Well, everyone's rushin' outside and only the girl's left. And the boy. And . . . Oh Lor'!'

'What? Has somethin' nasty happened to the girl?' Gran prompted him as Ruby gasped.

'Someone's nabbed her, Gran. They're carryin' her away. She's strugglin', but it's no use.'

'What's happened to her?' asked Ruby.

'How do I know?' retorted Jem.

Gran gave him a sharp kick on the shin.

'Oh . . . I mean, yeh, course I know. The girl, she's . . . er . . . she's . . .'

'Not the girl – the woman, the woman who came runnin' in!' shrieked Ruby. 'What's happened to her? Is she in danger?'

'Well . . . er . . . well, yeh, I can see her quite clearly. She's runnin'. Yeh, she's running away from the crushers. But it's no use. They've caught her. They've taken her to clink . . . and now she's in court . . . and the beak . . . Oh Lor', the beak's put on his black cap and . . . and now they're . . . Crimes!'

'What?' Ruby sprang up, overturning her chair, her eyes wide with terror. 'What're they doin' to her? Tell me! Tell me!'

'They're stringin' her up.' Jem mimed a noose being looped around someone's neck. 'She's dead.'

'Dead?' Gran frowned. 'What did she say before she went?'

'Nothin'.'

'She must have said somethin'.'

'Nah, she didn't.'

'I reckon you must be comin' out of your trance, you ninny. Keep lookin' at this,' said Gran, waving the bit of glass in front of his eyes again. 'Maybe it'll get your brain workin'.'

'Oh right . . . Yeh . . . Yeh, that woman did say

somethin'. Just before she popped her clogs, she said, "Lawks a mercy, if only I'd gone to the crushers and told them everythin' . . ."' Another sharp kick from Gran. 'Nah. Nah, not the crushers, I meant the gypsy. She said, "If only I'd told that old gypsy woman what happened to the little girl I wouldn't be hangin' here now on the end of a rope."'

But Jem's words fell on deaf ears, for Ruby had fainted.

'Now look what you've done, upsettin' her with all that mumbo-jumbo,' grumbled the Prehistoric Man, picking up the stricken woman and rocking her in his arms. 'Pack off, the pair of you. Tellin' people's fortunes is a crime anyway. You should be ashamed of yourselves, makin' a livin' out of cheatin'. Lor',' he huffed indignantly, 'I can't believe the things some people'll do for money.'

22

Their heads down, their feet pounding the ground, Ned and Billy finally escaped from the crowd but a woman running from the opposite direction collided with them with a bone-shattering smack! As she fell flat on her back, crying, 'Cor, love a duck!' her skirt over her head, her legs akimbo, Ned tripped over her feet and Billy fell flat on her chest, knocking the breath out of her lungs.

'Oy!' she yelled.

In struggling to get up Ned ripped yet another hole in the woman's very ragged shawl.

'Now look what you've done! You've ruined it, you little . . .! Billy? Ned?'

'Ma!'

The boys didn't know whether to throw their arms around their mother's neck or run for their lives.

'You half killed me, you little varmints,' she fumed, getting painfully to her feet.

'Sorry, Ma,' said Ned, backing away nervously, for his mother in a rage could inflict more damage in five seconds than Ahmed the Assassin in five rounds.

'Where've you been? What've you been doin'? I've chased all over this ruddy fair after you boys.' She stopped and looked round. 'Where's Jem? Why isn't he with you?'

'We don't know where he is, Ma,' said Ned.

'He's run away,' said Billy.

'Run away?' Ma's face darkened. 'Why did he do that?'

'Cos we were in the freak show . . .'

'Watchin' the Pirate . . .'

'And we met Clara, the girl that was in the work-house with us . . .'

'And she gave Jem her bonnet and gloves and neckerchief. Real jammy they were, Ma.'

Ma's face changed from horror to rage, and before Ned could duck she gave him a whack around the ear. 'You're gettin' as bad as Jem,' she stormed. 'I get nothin' but whim-wham from him. And now you. Worryin' me like that. I thought it was true for a moment. As if that poor little mite would have a jammy bonnet and gloves and a neckerchief,' she scoffed. 'She'd be lucky if she had two potato skins to rub together.'

'It's not rubbish, Ma. It's true. Her ma's married a man that's filthy rich. She's a real lady now.'

'She gave Jem the stuff, Ma. She did. I saw her,' insisted Billy.

'But everyone thought Jem'd stolen it from her . . .'

'And when they couldn't find Clara . . .'

'They thought he'd kidnapped her . . .'

'So Jem took off . . .'

'And they all started chasin' him . . .'

'And what if he gets copped, Ma?' said Ned, anxiety gnawing at him. 'What if the crushers catch him?'

'Nah, Jem's a clever kid – he wouldn't let the crushers cop him,' said Ma, who for all her bluster was secretly very proud of her eldest son. 'Come on,' she said, taking Billy's hand, 'let's go back to our pitch. Ten to one Jem's already there.'

23

Clara had grown used to the sound of the waves lapping against the sides of *La Gaviota* and the constant rocking motion and she fell asleep. As the terrifying memory of her kidnapping slipped away, the girl dreamed she was home again, in the house in Victoria Square, lying in a soft bed, her mother bending over her, smiling, murmuring . . .

'*¡Despierta, niña!* Wake up!'

Clara opened her eyes in alarm A woman was bending over her – not her mother, not that sweet, loving face, but another, harsh, cruel. The realization of where she was, the cramped locker, the stifling heat, hit Clara so hard that her eyes filled with tears. But she would not cry, she determined, clenching her jaw. She would never let that she-devil see how frightened she was.

The woman reached down, put her hand under Clara's shoulders and yanked her upright.

'Is your supper,' she said, indicating the bowl in

her other hand. 'Open your mouth. Open your mouth, I say . . . *En seguida* . . . Now!' she barked.

Eyeing the grey, gluey gruel, Clara reluctantly opened her mouth and the woman ladled some in. Clara had almost forgotten how disgusting gruel was. In her new home she ate delicious things, like hot pies and baked potatoes and gooseberry tart and fig pudding. She pulled a face when she swallowed the gruel and the woman burst out laughing.

'You no like? *Qué lástima* – a pity. But you eat!' And forcing Clara's mouth open, she spooned in another large helping.

Clara made a gurgling noise as if she was choking.

'What wrong?' The woman bent down, looking at her anxiously. 'What wrong with you?'

Clara waited until the woman's face was close to hers, then she spat – with all her might. The gruel splattered in the woman's eyes and trickled stickily down her nose and cheeks.

The woman shrieked and began swearing at Clara in a torrent of Spanish.

'*¿Qué pasa, Matilde?* What's happening?' A man's head appeared in the hatchway and grabbing the woman and pinning her arms to her sides, he pulled her away.

'*Let me get at her, Paco! ¡Voy a matarla!*' shrieked the woman, struggling to free herself. 'I kill her!'

'*¿And how're we going to get the money if she's dead?*' snarled the man. '*¡No sea estupida, Matilde!*' And haranguing her loudly, he hauled the irate woman away and slammed and locked the door behind him.

Clara lay back, grinning. She was glad she'd spat the gruel in the wretched woman's face. And she would do it again, she thought, laughing out loud at the prospect. She would do it again and again, for as long as they held her captive.

24

Gran and Jem hid behind the freaks' tent, taking it in turns to peek round the side.

'D'you think Ruby's ever comin' out?' said Jem, growing impatient.

'Yeh, she'll come. She's just waitin' till the coast's clear before she makes a run for it.'

'A run where?'

'That's what we'll find out,' said Gran. 'She's frightened, no doubt about it. She believed every word you said. You did a good job, son.'

'Yeh, I'm a stunnin' actor . . . Oh, look, there she is,' said Jem, as Ruby came out of the tent and looked nervously around.

'Right,' said Gran, as the woman took off. 'Don't let her out of your sight, Jem. Stay close.'

Jem started to run, but he quite forgot he was wearing a long skirt and it wrapped itself around his legs, tripping him up.

'Dratted thing!' he swore, struggling to his feet.

'Hold it up, Jem, like this,' said Gran, taking her skirt in both hands and drawing it up.

Following Ruby was not easy, for time and again she glanced over her shoulder so Jem and Gran had to dodge into a booth or behind a stall, and the crowd was so dense that often they couldn't see her.

'Keep up, Gran,' Jem urged her. 'She's goin' in the park . . . Oh, she's fallen over,' he said, as Ruby barged into a man and fell flat on her back.

'Look where you're goin', missus. It's no good runnin' forward and lookin' backward,' he said angrily.

'Sorry. I'm s-sorry, guv,' stammered Ruby, scrambling to her feet. And away she went again, across the broad field at the entrance to the park and up one of the steep slopes at the side.

'Faster, Gran, Lor's sake!' Jem cried. 'Faster or we'll lose her.'

'It's no use,' said the old woman, sinking to the ground. 'You go. I'll wait here. And Jem,' she called after him as he sped away, holding his skirt up with one hand and his bonnet on with the other, 'be careful. Don't do nothin' silly. Just see where she goes . . .' But Jem was already halfway up the hill and didn't hear his grandmother's words of warning.

On ran Ruby until she reached one of the

traders' caravans and stumbling up the steps she pounded on the door, screaming, 'Jake! Jake! Let me in. For the love of God, let me in!'

Jem crept behind a tree and crouched low, watching.

A man opened the door and Ruby flung herself at him, crying, 'They're after me, Jake. The crushers. They're after me.'

'Crushers?' The man frowned. 'I don't see no crushers.'

'They know all about us, Jake. They know. A gypsy girl told me. Said I'd be strung up for what we've done.' The woman's voice rose hysterically. 'We've got to get away from here. We've got to go now. Now!'

'Gypsies, pah! What do they know?' The man scoffed. 'We did the job and we're stayin' here till we get the money. Now get in and stop your caterwaulin',' he said, pushing her roughly into the caravan. And with a quick look round to make sure he wasn't observed, he shut the door.

Jem ran back down the hill twice as fast as he'd run up it, almost falling over in his haste to get back to Gran.

'Well?' she said eagerly. 'Where did she go? Who did she see?'

'A man – in a caravan,' Jem said, beside himself with excitement. 'A man with a black patch over his eye and a wooden leg and a hook where his hand should be.'

25

The task of tracking down the Snake had been entrusted to Detective Inspector Craddock. A quietly efficient man, who had been with the Metropolitan Police since the inception of the Detective Branch in 1842, Craddock had solved some tough crimes, such as the theft of Lady Eden's sapphire necklace and Lady FitzHubert's diamond tiara, but bringing the Snake to justice was proving much harder, so hard that Craddock was beginning to think the man must have magical powers.

Nevertheless, he was determined to capture him. Craddock had a reputation. He had never failed. 'Always gets his man,' they said admiringly of him. But weariness was taking its toll. Craddock badly needed a break from his arduous routine. Unfortunately for him, policemen never got a break. They worked every day, even Christmas Day. But they were allowed one week's leave a year, unpaid.

'If I could have a week's leave, sir,' he said to his commanding officer, a gruff ex-colonel by the name of Hamilton-Harley, who had fought under Wellington at Waterloo and Corunna.

'*What?*' Hamilton-Harley had brought with him from his various campaigns a fearsome reputation for working his men and horses into the ground. 'Out of the question,' he barked.

'Just one day then, if you'd be so kind, sir. I know my wife and children would be most pleased. They hardly ever see me.'

Resisting the temptation to observe that his own children were more than happy not to see their crusty old father, Hamilton-Harley reluctantly agreed.

Craddock's wife and ten-year-old John and nine-year-old Susannah were indeed delighted with the news.

'Dad, would you take us to Greenwich fair?' said John.

'Oh yes, please, please, Dad. We've never been,' said Susannah.

Craddock's heart sank. All he wanted to do was sit in his favourite armchair all day smoking a pipe and reading *The Times*. He looked beseechingly at his wife, but there was no help from that quarter.

'It would be nice, dear,' she said. 'The children haven't had an outing for a long time.'

'It's true, Dad,' agreed his daughter, climbing on to his lap and putting her arms around his neck. 'We haven't been anywhere. And we've been ever so good, haven't we, Mum?'

Craddock sighed. 'All right,' he nodded.

'Could we go by steamer, Dad?' said John.

'That's a good idea,' agreed Craddock. 'Let's go on the river.'

'But boats . . .' shuddered his wife, who was mortally afraid of any vehicle not drawn by horses.

'Are perfectly safe, my dear,' he said.

In his youth Craddock had been to the fair many times but that, he thought wistfully, had been years ago and he had quite forgotten how deafening the noise was, how pungent the smell of fried fish and pickled onions, how dense the crowds as they strolled along the streets lined with stalls and sideshows. And then there was Greenwich Park, normally a place of such tranquillity, now crammed with all manner of entertainments, not least of which was the dubious sport of running flat out from the top of the hill to the bottom, resulting in many a bloodied nose and bruised rib.

Craddock quickly realized that a day at the fair meant, as far as his children were concerned, a day in which he continually dipped into his pocket for yet another penny ice or lollipop or donkey ride or a look through a telescope – 'Dad, I can see St Paul's Cathedral . . . and Epping Forest and . . . Oh –' squeals of delight – 'I can see a woman over there hanging her washing on the line!'

As the day wore on Craddock's thoughts turned longingly to home, a quiet supper, a pipe or two and then bed. Ignoring the children's protests that they hadn't seen the marionette show or been to the theatre, he took them firmly by the hand and led them away. But Mrs Craddock was intrigued by a crowd that had gathered around a tree, gabbling excitedly.

'Dora, please . . .' exclaimed Craddock.

'I'll just be a moment,' she said. 'I want to see what all the fuss is about.'

'And if it's a fight?'

'Oh, I'm sure it isn't. It all seems very amicable, dear.'

Craddock waited with mounting impatience while his wife gently but firmly eased her way through to the front of the crowd to see what they were staring at.

'Well?' said Craddock, when she returned.

'There's a notice attached to the tree. Nobody could read so I read it for them.'

'That's very civil of you, Dora. And what exactly did it say? Has someone lost their pet dog?'

'No, a little girl – kidnapped. The police are looking for someone to help them with their enquiries. He has the strangest name.' She laughed. 'Perkin*ski*. Can you imagine it? Perkin*ski* . . . Is something wrong, my dear?' she asked anxiously, for her husband, who had ambled around the fair all day trying in vain to hide his boredom and could barely wait to get home, had now sprung to life like one of the jack-in-the-boxes for sale on the toy stalls.

'Perkinski?' he said. 'Which one – Bert, Arthur, Ted, Nick, Percy, Jim, Sid, Fred, Ben, George, Billy, Ned, Jem . . .?'

'The boy's name is Jem.'

'I might have known it. Where there's trouble there's a Perkinski – and Jem's the worst of the lot. Take the children home. I will follow later. But don't be disturbed if I'm not back tonight.'

'But, my dear, you are supposed to be resting.'

'And I shall, Dora,' Craddock reassured her, 'after I've collared Jem Perkinski.'

26

As darkness fell a young couple crept into the bushes and sat down within a few feet of where Slithe was hiding. Startled, he woke with a hiss, unwound and slithered away.

All was quiet now. The Thames gleamed silver in the moonlight and the treetops moved gently in the evening breeze. Everyone had gone to the fair. Slithe could see the distant lights and hear the raucous music from the hurdy-gurdies and round-abouts, the brass bands going oom-pah-pah, the people in the swingboats screaming with fear and delight as they swung higher and higher until it seemed they would go right over the top, the tradesmen barking their wares, the showmen cajoling people to 'Roll up! Roll up!'

A shadow passed over the moon and Slithe scowled, his thin lips curling back over teeth, sharp, yellow. 'Who's there?' he hissed, his dagger at the ready.

'Slithe.' A disembodied voice came from the shadows surrounding him.

'Oh, it's you, Master. Begging your pardon.'

'You have the girl safe?'

'Safe and sound, Master. They'll never find her, no matter how hard they look.'

'You were seen.'

'No. No, I was careful. I waited till everyone had left the booth, just like you said, before I took her. I—'

'You were careless.' The voice rose in anger. 'Not everyone had left. There was a boy still there. He is a danger to us. He could ruin everything.'

'I'm sorry, Master. I'm real sorry.' Slithe inched forward on his belly as if he was about to lick the man's feet.

'His name is Jem Perkinski.'

'Jem Perkinski,' Slithe repeated, curling his tongue around the name like a lizard swallowing a helpless insect.

'Find him.'

'I will, Master.'

'Kill him.'

'Yes, Master.'

27

'There are always a number of felonies committed at the fair each year, principally of the theft variety, the location and magnitude of the numbers attending being a magnet for every pickpocket from here to Timbuktu,' Superintendent Blake said to Craddock, who had made his way directly to the Greenwich police station when he heard about Clara. 'Then, of course, there are other undesirables, such as the drunk and disorderly. But I regard the abduction of a young girl, especially the daughter of as highly respected a member of the community as Mr Sterling, to be particularly reprehensible.'

'Surely the abduction of any child, whether she be the daughter of a beggar or a baronet is always wrong, sir,' said Craddock.

'Indeed so, inspector,' said Blake, although, from his expression, he clearly thought the baronet's child took precedence over the beggar's.

'Has there been any sighting of Jem Perkinski, sir?'

'Not as yet. But be assured we shall have him before the day is out. The rest of his family are here, and since they are all scoundrels there can be little doubt that they are involved in this dastardly crime.'

Craddock frowned. 'I must confess it does not sound like their kind of crime. Petty theft, yes. Horse stealing, certainly. Cheating and tricking the public, most definitely. But kidnapping . . .? Then again, perhaps the prospect of making a great deal of money rather than a few pennies was something they couldn't resist.'

'I think you have hit the nail upon the head, inspector,' said Blake. 'It is my intention, therefore, to apprehend them and bring them in for question-ing . . . Ah, Mrs Sterling,' he said, getting to his feet as Clara's mother came in with her husband on one side and Mr Mallick on the other, supporting her.

'No news?' she asked in a faint voice. 'No news of my Clara?'

'I regret not, madam. But permit me to intro-duce Detective Inspector Craddock from Scotland Yard. He has expressed a keen interest in the crime.'

'I have a personal knowledge of one of the

suspects,' explained Craddock, 'which I consider might be of use to the Greenwich police in their investigations.'

'You think it will help find my little girl?'

'I very much hope so.'

'Pray sit down, madam. You must be weary,' said Blake, motioning her to a chair.

'We have searched for Clara everywhere,' said Mr Sterling, who looked on the point of collapse himself.

'We've asked people if they've seen her but they all say no. They don't care,' said his wife bitterly. 'Long as *their* kids are safe, they don't care. Course, if there was money in it . . .'

'An excellent idea, Florence,' said Mr Sterling. 'Superintendent, would you let it be known that there is a fifty – no, a hundred-pound reward for the person who finds or helps us to find Clara?'

Craddock's mouth fell open. A hundred pounds was as much as he earned in a year. Even the superintendent looked surprised. 'That is very generous, sir,' he said.

'I would willingly give more. I would give all I possess to have Clara back,' said Mr Sterling as his wife wept, hiding her face in a handkerchief.

'May I suggest you go home,' said Blake, laying a

comforting hand on her shoulder. 'There is nothing more you can do here. If we receive any news we shall inform you of it immediately.'

'Thank you, superintendent,' said Mr Sterling. 'Come, Florence,' he said, helping the weeping woman to her feet. 'I feel we are leaving this investigation in safe hands.'

'I have a request, sir,' said Craddock when the Sterlings had gone. 'Although, of course, I am not officially assigned to the case, I should be most grateful if you would permit me to interview the Perkinskis. I have, shall we say, a close – unfortunately far too close – acquaintance with most of them that might be of value.'

'I have no objection to that.' Barker nodded. 'I shall arrange for you to question them as soon as my constables have brought them in.'

28

As Ma and the boys got closer to their pitch on the very edge of the park they knew that something was wrong. Whenever the Perkinskis got together there was always a great deal of jollity, what with the incessant chattering and chuckling and Uncle Nick playing the violin and Uncle Percy doing the sailor's hornpipe and Gran doing a wild fandango and Kate singing. But now there were only cries of dismay and angry shouts.

'What's happenin', Ma?' Billy said in his piping voice.

'Shh!' She put a hand over his mouth. 'You stay here with Ned. I'll go and see.' And scuttling from one clump of bushes to the next she reached the top of an incline from where, hiding behind the broad trunk of a horse chestnut, she had a good view of the site.

Such a sorry scene met her eyes that she inadvertently cried out, 'Hell and Tommy!' for all the

Perkinskis in sight had been rounded up like cattle by a dozen or more constables, who were brandishing their truncheons and shouting, 'Go quietly now! Move along there! No trouble or you'll regret it.'

'But we haven't done nothin' wrong,' protested Uncle Arthur.

'It isn't fair,' said Auntie Maud.

'You're always pickin' on us.'

'Leave us alone.'

But their protests, though long and loud, had no effect and chivvied by the policemen they shuffled away, scowling and muttering dire oaths against 'varminty crushers'.

'Where're they takin' them, Ma?' whispered Ned, who with Billy had crept up behind her.

'To the lock-up, I reckon.'

'Why?'

'How do I know?'

'D'you think it's somethin' to do with Jem?'

'I wouldn't be surprised.' His mother sighed. 'It's always somethin' to do with Jem.'

'I didn't see him, Ma.'

'Nor me.'

'So what're we goin' to do?'

'I don't know. What with your pa in hospital and Jem on the run and now this . . .' She nodded at the little campsite, empty now, the fire dying down, the water in the cooking pots turning cold, a few stray dogs sniffing around in the hope of finding some scraps. 'I don't know which way to turn and that's the truth.'

'Gran could help us, Ma,' suggested Ned. 'She could look in her crystal ball and tell us what to do.'

'Perhaps she could, son,' Ma nodded. 'But we don't know where Gran is, do we?'

'She's probably in clink too,' suggested Billy brightly, 'or on her way to Australie.'

29

Convinced that Craddock was going to arrest them for their various money-making activities, the Perkinskis invented stories so patently absurd that the inspector didn't know whether to laugh or cry.

'I was just walkin' along, mindin' my business, when I looked down and . . . by jingo, there was this pile of coins just layin' there! How was I to know they were fakes, guv?' said Ted, emptying his pockets of a dozen or more forged guineas.

'This pesky poodle kept followin' me around so I picked it up and put it somewhere safe and then this woman came lookin' for it and when I told her I'd got it she was so pleased she made me take five quid as a reward . . . Well, I couldn't say no, could I, guv?' said Uncle Bill.

'I was linin' up for a dish of pickled whelks when the woman in front turned round and said her arms had gone all funny like so would I put my hand in her pocket and get out her purse so she could buy some whelks . . . I had to help the poor thing, didn't I, guv?' said Cousin Em.

'I have not come to hear your confessions,' said Craddock with increasing exasperation. 'I am conducting an investigation into the abduction of Clara Sterling.'

'Who?'

'Before her mother's marriage, she was known as Clara Forbes.'

'Was she?'

'She used to live in Seven Dials.'

'Did she?'

'And she now resides in Victoria Square.'

'She does what?'

'She *lives* in Victoria Square.'

'Does she?

'Oh, for goodness' sake . . .!'

'It's my opinion the Perkinskis are much too stupid to have committed a crime of this magnitude,' Superintendent Blake said to Craddock over a reviving cup of tea.

'I agree with you, sir. This is the work of a far more sophisticated gang, and Jem Perkinski was somehow caught up as – although I am loath to use

the word when referring to that little rogue – an *innocent* bystander.'

The superintendent sighed. 'I suppose I must let them all go.'

'There is certainly no reason to detain them,' said Craddock, 'but it does seem unchristian to let them loose on the poor, unsuspecting folk visiting the fair, so may I suggest you wait until tomorrow and release them with a stern warning.'

'A stern warning about what precisely?'

'About whatever they're about to do.'

'Which is what?'

'Something illegal, sir. You can be sure of that.'

30

Clara was used to the stench of London streets – the refuse piled high in every alleyway and courtyard, the mounds of horse and cattle dung, the rotting corpses of dogs, cats, rats and sometimes even babies lying in the gutter – but the smell from the river was much worse. The mighty Thames, which had once been so clean that swans floated on its surface and fish swam beneath, had now become nothing but a long, wide open sewer. The contents of every latrine and cesspit in the city flowed into it, turning the water brown and sludgy. To this was added the blood and butchered remains from the slaughter-houses and the waste from hospitals, knackers' yards, chemical and gas works and tanners.

Over and above this irksome stink Clara detected something else. She wrinkled her nose, sniffing the air. There was a sweet but sharp smell, one that she was familiar with and yet could not place. Not fish, not tobacco, not spices . . . Oranges! Of course – it was the smell that came from the oranges piled high on the costermongers' carts as they trundled along the streets of London.

An orange . . . Her mouth watered at the thought of it. She would have given anything for a sweet, juicy orange instead of the filthy grey gruel the woman had forced down her throat.

As night drew on, the last remaining chink of light disappeared and the walls of the chain locker closed in on her, suffocating her. How long would she be there? she wondered. What if? — her heart skipped a beat — What if her new father couldn't pay the ransom? What if he *wouldn't* pay the ransom? But he would. He would! He loved her . . . didn't he?

Tears stung her eyes but she blinked them away angrily. She had been in worse danger than this, she thought. As a crossing sweeper she had risked her life many times darting in and out of the traffic to clear away horse droppings and mud so that a lady or gentleman could cross the street without dirtying their shoes. She had been beaten in the workhouse and chased through the sewers by a mad, murderous workhouse master. But she had survived. And she would go on surviving, she thought, jutting out her chin. Someone would find her, someone would come and rescue her. Until then she would be brave.

She started to sing, softly at first, then louder and louder, a cheerful tune, 'Cherry ripe! Cherry ripe! Come and buy . . .' She had heard a small beggar girl singing it in the days when she lived in the rookery.

'¡Cállate!' growled a man. 'Shut you mouth or I shut it with my fist.'

'*Noisy brat!*'

Clara recognized the second voice, even though she couldn't understand the words. It was the woman Matilde.

'*The sooner we're rid of her the better.*'

31

Mr Sterling returned to Victoria Square in the early evening with his wife who, despite her exhaustion, refused to take to her bed. Instead she sat, rocking baby Pip in her arms and murmuring in his ear, 'They won't get you, my little treasure. I won't let them get you, my pet.'

There was a knock on the drawing-room door and Mrs Restall, the housekeeper, came in. It was obvious from her grey face and red-rimmed eyes that she too was deeply distressed, for in the short time she had known Clara she had become very fond of her.

'Is there anything I can get for you, sir?' she asked. 'Some kippered salmon, perhaps, or mutton chops, broiled kidneys . . .?'

'No, Mrs Restall, no supper for me, thank you. Florence . . .?' He looked at his wife enquiringly.

She shook her head and buried her tear-stained face in Pip's shoulder.

'Rose, Maisie and I want to say how sorry we are about Miss Clara, sir,' began the housekeeper, but she was interrupted by a loud rat-tat! on the front door.

'Who the devil is that?' said Mr Sterling irritably. 'Tell Rose I have no wish to receive any visitors this evening.'

'I will, sir,' said Mrs Restall but just as she was leaving the room the maid came to the door and said, 'If you please, sir, there's a Detective Inspector Craddock to see you.'

Mr Sterling, who had been standing by the fireplace, his hand resting on the mantel, his head bowed, almost ran across the room.

'My dear sir,' he said eagerly, as the maid ushered Craddock into the drawing room, 'have you found Clara? Is she all right? Is she . . . ?'

The words died on his lips as Craddock shook his head.

'I regret I have nothing to report, sir. And you'll forgive my intrusion at this late hour, but I have some questions . . .' He glanced at Mrs Sterling, who was clutching Pip and looking at him with an agonized expression. 'I felt it was not appropriate to put them to you at Greenwich. It would have fatigued Mrs Sterling unnecessarily.'

'That is most considerate of you,' said Mr Sterling. 'Florence, my dear, why don't you take the baby into the garden for a while. The cool air will help calm your nerves.' And kissing her tenderly on the forehead, he led her to the door.

'Do you truly have nothing to tell me?' he said to Craddock when she had gone.

'Nothing, sir. I'm sorry.'

'But the reward — a hundred pounds — a not inconsiderable sum of money . . . I felt sure that would have encouraged some response.'

'Not as yet, sir. We can only hope that it will loosen someone's tongue in time.'

'Hope,' sighed Mr Sterling, passing a weary hand across his eyes. 'I am fast losing hope, inspector . . . Oh, I do beg your pardon,' he said, realizing that Craddock was still standing. 'Pray, have a seat. Will you take a glass of sherry?'

'That would be most acceptable, sir. Thank you,' said Craddock, settling himself in a large, over-stuffed armchair, its head and legs elaborately, if not grotesquely carved. Indeed every piece of wood in the room, from the vast dresser to the piano, tables, chairs and doors of cupboards and cabinets, was covered in vines, grapes, flowers, fruit and animals.

While Mr Sterling poured two glasses of fine

Spanish sherry from a cut-glass decanter, Craddock looked about him, nodding in silent admiration, for the drawing room was a superior version of the one in his own home, which Dora called the parlour, a room decorated in the most sombre colours, from the purple-embossed wallpaper to the dark green curtains.

Craddock ran his eyes over the vast assortment of ornaments that cluttered every surface. Dora did not allow John and Susannah into the parlour except when there were visitors, and then the children were expected to sit quietly, without speaking, unless spoken to, their hands on their knees so as not to accidentally touch or — God forbid! — break any of the lamps or vases or china figurines. Craddock wondered if Mr Sterling ever permitted Clara and baby Pip to play in his drawing room. They would certainly have had much to look at, he thought, not least the large collection of stuffed animals and birds under glass domes.

As if he had read the inspector's thoughts Mr Sterling said, 'Clara has spent many a happy hour in here. She takes such delight in living creatures, especially birds. Such a sweet, innocent child, inspector. It breaks my heart to think of her in the

174

clutches of those . . . those . . .' He clenched his fists and turned away to hide his emotion.

'Is there anyone you suspect of having abducted Clara?'

'Certainly not.'

'Your relatives . . . ?'

'An uncle so ill he never leaves his bed, and two nieces, maiden ladies of unimpeachable character.'

'And your friends?'

'I have a very small circle of friends and even fewer acquaintances, since until my marriage my work dominated my life. But I will vouch for the integrity of all of them.'

'And what of your business colleagues?'

'Everyone in my employ has been with me for many, many years. They are all loyal, devoted servants. As for Septimus Mallick, he joined the company from school as a junior clerk, and by dint of hard work and boundless enthusiasm increased the scope and volume of the business so considerably that I made him a junior partner a short time ago.'

'I imagine he comes from a modest background?'

'On the contrary, inspector. His father was a major in the Dragoon Guards. Unfortunately he spent rather too much time at the gaming tables and lost all his money, which meant that young Septimus and his mother had a hard time of it. However, a short while ago Septimus's aunt died. She was a wealthy widow with no children, and though she left some of her money to charitable institutions, I understand Septimus inherited the bulk of her estate. To be frank, inspector, when he informed me of the legacy I greatly feared that he would leave me and set up on his own but, God be praised, that has not happened. I do not know what I would do without him.'

'And what of your wife, sir?'

'I rather suspected that was the reason you did not want to question me in her presence,' said Mr Sterling, bristling with indignation. 'I can assure you although my wife has not enjoyed the benefits of a privileged upbringing, she is a most honourable lady.'

'I don't doubt that for one minute,' said Craddock, 'but you surely understand that there are questions of some delicacy I can't put to her without distressing her.'

'Of course, of course. Forgive me, inspector. I am overwrought. The terrible events of this day are preventing me from acting and thinking rationally. Ask me what you will.'

'I should like to know about your wife's relatives.'

'She has a younger brother, Bob, a fine young man in Her Majesty's navy.'

'And what of her other relatives?'

'To my knowledge she has none. Certainly she has never spoken of any. As for friends . . . She lived in Seven Dials, but since our wedding she has never returned. I have told her I should be delighted to welcome her former acquaintances to my house, but she always declines. I think Seven Dials and its inhabitants hold too many painful memories of poverty and illness for her.'

'She must be the happiest woman in London now, living in such a pleasing house with a benevolent gentleman such as yourself,' smiled Craddock.

'I think she is . . . That is to say, I think she was happy. But of late . . .'

'Yes?'

'Something is troubling her. She never speaks of it to me and I am reluctant to press her. And . . .' Again Mr Sterling hesitated. 'It is probably just a foolish fancy, inspector, but I have had the feeling for some time that something, someone, evil is close by, casting a shadow over this house.'

32

Just as Kate had predicted, her boyfriend, Henry, and his partner, Shep, had been up and down the river all day, ferrying revellers to and from the fair, and as darkness fell the two young watermen slumped over their oars, exhausted.

'I'm dead beat,' said Henry.

'Me too,' said Shep. 'But we've taken a tidy sum today, more than we take in a month normal like. And there's still tomorrow and the day after.'

'And the fair'll be back next week. That's another three days. We'll be rich, Shep.' Henry rubbed his hands and laughed. 'We'll be able to give up workin' and live like some of the gen'lemen we get in this boat, with their fancy clothes and . . .'

'Their fine gold watches,' sniggered Shep, taking one out of his pocket and swinging it under Henry's nose.

'Where'd you get that? Did you nick it?' said

Henry, flaring up. 'I thought we'd agreed there'd be no more stealin'. If we get caught . . .'

'Don't worry, we won't. By the time that old codger realizes his watch has gone —' he nodded at the back of their last customer as he headed towards the fair — 'he won't know where he lost it or who nicked it.'

'All the same,' Henry fumed, 'we made an agreement and you broke it. I'm tellin' you, Shep,' he bent forward, wagging a finger in the other boy's face, 'I don't want to end up in clink or boated to some country the other side of the world like your old man. I've got a job. I've got my girl. And I don't want you goin' and spoilin' it all.'

'All right, all right, don't get your shirt out,' said Shep, turning surly. 'I won't do it again.'

'You said that last time. And the time before.' Henry's eyes flashed fire.

'But this was such easy pickin's, 'Enry. The watch was hangin' out of the bloke's pocket. It was beggin' me to take it.'

'Tell that to the magistrate, you stupe!'

'I've told you, I won't do it again.'

'That a promise?'

'Cross my heart—'

'And hope to lie. Yeh, the number of times I've heard that,' said Henry, as Shep laughed.

'Come on, let's go to the Crown and Anchor. I need a pint or three after all that rowin'.'

'You go ahead. I'll catch you up.'

'Ta-ta, then,' said Shep and he strutted away on his bandy legs.

Henry watched him go with a mixture of affection and irritation. He had known Shep all his life, had grown up with him. When they were eleven they had both been apprenticed to a freeman of the Company of Watermen and Lightermen to learn their trade. For Henry Chivers it had been easy. The freeman, or master, was his father and he had grown up on the Thames, knew all about boats, could practically row before he could walk. The river was in his blood. The Chivers had been watermen for as long as anyone could remember, right back to the days of Shakespeare, so it was said.

Shep was different. His father had been a lighterman who had supplemented his meagre income with stolen goods. The police had caught him so often leaving the docks in the dead of night with a stash of tobacco or brandy pilfered from a ship that the magistrates, having repeatedly fined and imprisoned him, finally lost patience and ordered him transported to one of Britain's colonies just a few weeks before his son was born.

Shep's mother had been a mudlark. She had spent her days wading through the mud left on the shore by the receding tide, bent double as she groped for anything that might bring her a penny or two – old iron, rope, bones, nails, coal. But standing up to her knees, and sometimes her waist, in freezing water all winter long had finally proved too much for her sickly body and she was found one morning, face down in the foul mire, still clutching her basket. Which left Shep an orphan when he was still a baby. And since Henry's father was a kind-hearted man, and he wanted a brother for his only child, he took him in.

The two boys quickly formed a strong bond, despite being completely unlike in both physique and temperament. Henry was quiet, thoughtful, clever. When he wasn't working he took his slate and chalks and sat at the water's edge sketching all that he saw – the steamers, ferries, sailing ships, barges, wherries and scullers, a forest of masts and sails as far as his eye could see; the loads and riggings, the black tarpaulins, the old coiled ropes and fenders; the dock labourers, ballast getters and lumpers – powerful men, tall, big-boned and muscular; the watermen, many of them dressed like sailors in pilot-jackets and canvas trousers, waiting for passengers at the foot of the stairs, some smoking, some dozing.

In his way, Shep was more typical of a waterman than Henry. Rough, unruly, witty, he always had to have the last word, no matter how rude that word was. Many a time Henry's father had taken the strap to him, but he could never quell the boy's indomitable spirit and more often than not, despite himself, he ended up laughing. What he didn't know, and it would have grieved him greatly if he had, was that Shep, like his father, was fast becoming a criminal.

While Henry sketched, Shep devoted his spare time to climbing aboard ships while their crew was ashore or at supper and going down into their cabins to steal whatever he could find. To make matters worse, he had taken to stealing from the passengers he and Henry ferried across the river.

Henry was beside himself the first time he saw Shep sliding a purse from the pocket of a woman's skirt and he had threatened to tell his father.

'We've two more years of our apprenticeship to go,' he had said. 'But if my dad finds out you're a thief, he'll cast you off.'

Shep had made light of it, protesting that it was the first time it had happened and would certainly be the last. But Henry had caught him thieving again and again.

The boy was incorrigible and Henry was at his wits' end.

'*Tell your father,*' insisted a small voice in his head that April evening as he stood on the jetty at Greenwich watching the sun set over the river. '*Get rid of him, or you'll end up in prison or worse and you'll lose all you've worked for. You'll never be a waterman.*'

'*And what use is a waterman?*' said another voice scathingly. '*They're no longer needed. Their trade is finished.*'

Henry's shoulders slumped. It was true. In olden times there had been thousands of watermen, but the coming of horse-drawn coaches and then steamboats and steam trains had put paid to most of them. Henry missed the thrill of 'shooting' through the narrow arches of the old bridge with its currents so treacherous that only a skilled waterman could pass. But since the opening of the new London Bridge in 1831, any fool in a tub could do it.

'That's the end of us,' said Henry's grandfather, who had died from the grief of it.

Henry only ever expected to make a meagre living from the river, but it was his home, his life, it was where he felt most at ease. And with Kate by his side . . . he smiled at the thought of her freckled face, her cheeky grin, her mass of bright red curls – he would be happy. As for Shep, he would give him one more chance. Just one more.

As he turned to go he heard a girl singing in a clear, sweet voice, 'Cherry ripe! Cherry ripe! Come and buy . . .' It was coming from one of the Spanish schooners. Suddenly a man shouted and the singing stopped.

'If only my Kate could sing like that, we could make a mint of money,' Henry thought ruefully, heading off to the dancing booth to meet her. 'But whenever she opens her mouth people put their hands over their ears and beg for mercy.'

33

Craddock stood on the steps of the Sterlings' residence, looking about him. The streets were empty, Victoria Square deserted. He knew he should go home; Dora and the children were waiting for him, but they would not be surprised if he did not return that night for, as his wife said, 'Once he gets a sniff of a villain, Dennis is like a bloodhound. He will not stop until he has tracked them down.'

And Craddock had got a sniff of a villain, the 'something evil' that was casting a shadow over Mr Sterling's house.

He set off down the street, walking with a brisk, purposeful gait, so that anyone watching would have assumed he was eager to get home. But when he reached Buckingham Palace Road he turned back and, scuttling from one pool of darkness to the next in the gaslit street, he approached Victoria Square again and, with a quick look to left and right, stole into a clump of prickly holly and laurel bushes from where he had a good view of the Sterlings' house. Taking off his top hat, which was strengthened with cane, he sat on it and settled down to wait.

34

Jem and Gran had been crouching behind a tree for some time, watching the Pirate's caravan.

'Lor', my screwmatics is killin' me,' complained the old lady, rubbing her aching knees. 'I can't stay here much longer, Jem.'

'You've got to, Gran. I'll wager Clara's in there, and you and me've got to get her out.'

'Yeh, well, you and me can't do it on our own. Tell you what, you cut back and tell your uncles we need their help. And Jem,' she called after him as he sped away, 'bring Cousin Annie too. She's strong as a navvy. I've seen her flatten many a man that crossed her.'

Jem ran back to their pitch as fast as he could, but when he got there his mother and brothers and Cousin Annie were sitting with woebegone expressions around an empty cooking pot suspended over a pile of cold ashes.

'What's up?' he cried. 'Where is everyone? Where's Pa and Uncle Arthur and Uncle Jim and—'

'Who're you?' demanded Cousin Annie, looking at him with deep suspicion.

'Come to pinch our stuff, have you?' said Ma, getting to her feet. 'Well, you can hook it, my girl, or I'll . . .!'

'Ma, it's me,' said Jem, backing away as she and Cousin Annie came towards him, their fists raised threateningly.

'What?'

'Me,' said Jem, pulling off his bonnet.

'Lawks a mercy!'

'What the devil . . .?'

Out of the corner of his eye Jem could see Ned and Billy nudging each other and sniggering, 'A skirt! He's wearin' a skirt. And a bodice. And a bonnet . . . Lor', isn't he a nice piece of goods!'

Jem decided he had more important things to do than give his brothers a good thumping, although he would certainly do so later, and he briefly explained to his mother and Cousin Annie why he was disguised as a girl – 'Cos they think I nabbed that girl,' he finished.

'Yeh, we know.' Cousin Annie nodded. 'Your name's on posters all over the fair. Everywhere I

went people were jabberin' about you — Jem Perkins*ki* — and that Clara somethin' or other.'

Jem was torn between two emotions — fear at the prospect of being hunted down, arrested and probably transported for a major crime, and pride at having his name on everyone's lips. Unfortunately he couldn't help smiling smugly at the thought, which enraged his mother.

'It's nothin' to look so pleased about,' she scolded him. 'It's cos of you your uncles and aunts and cousins've been copped. The crushers think all us Perkinskis are in it.'

'But I keep tellin' you, Ma, I didn't do nothin',' protested Jem. 'I saw the bloke that did it — leastways I think it was a bloke.'

'Come on then,' said Cousin Annie, taking him firmly by the arm. 'You can explain to them crushers it was Clara what gave you her bonnet and gloves and you had nothin' to do with her bein' nabbed.'

'Don't be soft!' Jem pulled away from her. 'They'll never believe me.'

'Jem's right. Them crushers never believe a word honest folks like us say,' said Ma. 'We've got to find that girl so's she can tell the crushers the truth herself.'

'The Pirate's got Clara in his caravan, Ma, I'm sure of it. All we've got to do is get her out.'

'Oh yeh?' She looked at him doubtfully. 'How?'

'I've got a real jammy idea.'

'What is it?'

'It's . . . er . . . Well . . . er . . .' Jem faltered. 'I'll tell you when we get there.'

35

Around midnight the crowds began to leave the fair. Sleepy children were piled into the backs of carts, and faithful old dobbins plodded through the dark streets of Deptford and Southwark, back to the tenement buildings and crowded hovels of St Giles and Seven Dials.

The fairground people snuffed out the flares, yawned and curled up under their stalls or staggered back to their caravans to snatch a few hours' rest before the dawn of yet another hard day.

'Right, you know what you've got to do?' whispered Jem as his family gathered round him.

'You nick the Pirate's horse,' said Ned, 'then I bang on his door and shout, "Someone's nicked your horse, guv!" and run away and hide. And when him and his missus come out . . .'

'They'll go lookin' for their horse . . .' said Ma.

'And when they've gone, your ma and me'll go in their caravan and grab Clara,' said Cousin Annie.

'And by the time they get back . . .'

'With the horse . . .'

'We'll all have scarpered . . .'

'With Clara.'

'Jammy!' beamed Jem.

'And I'll stay here and keep Billy quiet,' said Gran.

'Don't let him get away, Gran,' Jem said, 'cos if he does he'll do somethin' sappy. He's always spoilin' our dodges.'

'I'll wallop him if he tries anythin',' said Gran, giving Billy a clip round the ear as a friendly warning.

'Right, I'm off,' whispered Jem. 'Count up to twenty, Ned, before you come.'

Ned frowned. 'I don't know how to count up to twenty.'

'Use your hands and feet, you stupe!'

'What d'you mean?'

'You've got five fingers on each hand,' explained Gran. 'And five toes on each foot. So if you count each one . . .'

'Oh yeh, I've tumbled to it. Hold on a minute, Jem, while I take my boots off.'

'Lor's sake!' fumed Jem.

'Right, I'm ready. Get goin',' said Ned, grasping the big toe of his left foot.

Jem, Ma and Cousin Annie crept out of their hiding place in the trees. While Ma and Cousin Annie went and hid behind the caravan, Jem scuttled across the clearing to where the Pirate's horse was tethered to a post. The moon was up, bathing the world in its brilliant light. Jem would have preferred a dark night, the sky thick with clouds, and time and again he looked round to make sure nobody was watching him. Making soft, soothing noises to the mare the way his cousin Sam, who was once a horse thief, had taught him, he undid the rope and pulled. But the mare refused to budge.

'Come on, beauty, come on,' Jem urged her.

The mare tossed her head and whinnied.

'Shh!' Jem stroked her nose, calming her. 'Shh, or they'll hear us.'

Frustrated by the mare's stubbornness, Jem made a final effort to move her. Digging in his heels and making a soft clicking noise with his tongue, he tugged as hard as he could. The mare reared up, snorting, and cantered away, her flying hooves narrowly missing the boy, who lost his balance and fell on his back with a loud cry.

'Oy!'

From his vantage point in the cleft of an oak tree Slithe heard the boy and woke with a hiss. Sliding out of his hiding place, his tongue darting in and out, in and out, he inched along a branch, watching . . .

'Go on, Ned. Go!' Gran whispered urgently in his ear.

'But I haven't got to the little toe of my right foot yet,' he protested.

'Go on, Lor's sake!' Gran said, giving him a push. 'Jem's in trouble.'

Ned raced down the slope and across the clearing, but just as he was about to clamber up the steps of the caravan the door flew open and Jake the Pirate stood there. His face took on a thunderous look when he saw his horse disappearing with Jem in hot pursuit and Ned staring up at him, wide-eyed with terror.

'What's happenin', Jake? Who's there?' cried Ruby, appearing in the doorway behind him. 'Is it the crushers?'

'Some scoundrels have nicked Jenny,' he said. 'Get him, Ruby.' He pointed at Ned, who was rooted to the spot. 'I'll go after the other.'

While the man went after Jem, Ruby lunged at Ned. Too late he regained his senses and turned to run, but she was on him, battening his arms behind his back and hauling him up the steps. Ned fought back, trying to wrap his legs around hers to trip her up, but she was a strong woman, toughened by years of hard work in the fair.

'Ma!' he shouted. 'Ma!'

His mother and Cousin Annie came running in time to see a screaming Ned being dragged into the caravan and the door slammed shut.

'Blimey, what was that?' cried Cousin Annie, ducking as a large bird flew over her head, squawking loudly.

'It's Joey!' cried Billy. And before Gran could stop him he ran out of their hiding place, shouting, 'It's the pirate's birdie. It's Joey!'

Slithe stopped, twisting back on himself with a half-sighing, half-hissing sound, watching the scene below – Jake away in the distance chasing Jem and the runaway horse, two women hammering on the door of the caravan, screaming and swearing, and a small boy . . . Slithe loathed children. He particularly loathed small boys, like the one in the huge cap and rolled up trousers that was running round in circles at the foot of the tree, laughing and shouting, 'Joey! Joey!'

The parrot landed on a branch close to Slithe, still squawking. Slithe looked at it malevolently. He hated birds as much as he hated children. His fingers itched to wring its neck but as he reached out with a scaly hand it screeched, 'Naughty boy! Pack off!' and flew to a higher branch.

'Joey!' cried Billy. 'Come here, Joey. Come to me.'

'Mud in your eye!' screeched the parrot.

'Damn that bird!' Slithe cursed. 'And damn the boy!'

The whole campsite was stirring now. Doors were opening, voices crying, 'What's up? What's the shindig?'

Slithe knew that in another moment the clearing would be filled with fairground people milling around. The Master would be displeased. He had wanted everything to be done quietly, secretly. The boy had to be silenced.

He glided back along the branch and round and down the tree trunk in one fluid movement until he reached the ground. But Billy was so busy staring up at the parrot and crying, 'Joey! Come here, Joey!' he

didn't see the man slithering towards him, and before he could shout for help his mouth was smothered by a foul-smelling hand.

36

Craddock crouched in the bushes, watching the Sterlings' house. Shortly before eleven all the lights had been extinguished, save for a room on the second floor which he presumed to be the Sterlings' bedroom. Poor wretches, he thought, for he knew the terrible anguish he and Dora would suffer if John or Susannah were kidnapped.

Although the day had been warm, the night was chill. A strong wind had replaced the gentle breeze, rattling chimney pots and bending trees. Craddock hunkered down, blowing on his hands to warm them. He would dearly have liked to get up, walk around, stamp his feet, get his blood circulating again, but he had to stay as quiet as he could if he was to catch the 'evil presence' Mr Sterling had spoken of. Was he wasting his time? he wondered. Was Mr Sterling a fanciful man who saw phantoms where there were only shadows? Certainly he seemed sensible, a down-to-earth businessman who . . . The light went off in the Sterlings' bedroom. Good, thought Craddock. It meant they were sleeping at last, or trying to.

A church clock chimed midnight. Craddock closed his eyes, running a weary hand over them. It had been a long day and he wished he too was in his bed, sunk in the warmth of a goose feather mattress under two or three heavy horsehair blankets. He did his best to fight off the wooziness in his head, but his chin moved closer and closer to his chest, his eyelids flickered and within minutes he was asleep. But part of his brain, probably the part that made him such a successful detective, stayed alert, nudging him awake an hour or so later.

'What? What?' he muttered, coming to with a startled grunt. What had woken him? he wondered. Was it a sound, a movement? Suddenly all his senses were alert. Someone, a heavily shrouded figure, had come out of the Sterlings' house, leaving the front door ajar, and was creeping down the steps. A woman – Craddock squinted, for the light from the gas lamps was not good and there were pools of darkness between them – a woman with her bonnet pulled so far down and her shawl wrapped up so high that even in the lamplight it was barely possible to see her face.

199

Craddock was deeply disappointed. He had hoped the evil presence that overshadowed the Sterlings' house was in some way connected to the kidnapping of little Clara. He had dreams of catching the criminal and hauling him back to Scotland Yard. But clearly this was just one of the maids stealing out under the cover of darkness to meet her young man. Although employers frowned on such behaviour and forbade their female servants to have followers, it happened all the time, even in the most respectable houses.

Craddock got to his feet, stretching his stiff legs and yawning hugely. He had wasted several hours of good sleeping time just to catch a servant girl. She had stolen into the square, looking furtively about her the whole time. A movement caught his eye, hers too, for she hurried towards it. A figure detached itself from the bushes. The woman opened her reticule and drew out what appeared to be a bundle of notes. The man – was it a man, Craddock could barely make him out? – snatched them from her.

Craddock was surprised. This was not the action of two lovers meeting illicitly. He had expected her to throw herself into the man's arms. Instead the two seemed to be arguing . . . He stole out of his

hiding place and crept towards them, using the bushes and trees as a cover, listening. He caught catches of their conversation, the woman's voice . . .

'I've given you enough. No more. I can't give you no more.'

'You fool!' the man hissed. 'D'you think you can get rid of me so easy?'

'But if Mr Sterling finds out . . .'

'If he finds out, you'll be ruined. I'll make sure of that.'

The man melted into the bushes and the woman turned and scurried back. As she passed close to where Craddock was hidden, he caught a glimpse of her face – the briefest glimpse, but in that instant he knew it wasn't Rose or Maisie, the Sterlings' young maids. The woman creeping up the steps of the house like a thief in the night was none other than Clara's mother.

37

'It's the crushers!' the cry went up across the campsite. In the twinkling of a bedpost the crowd melted away as three policemen came running into the clearing, springing their rattles.

'Stop that!' said one to Ma and Cousin Annie, who were still pounding on the door of the Pirate's caravan, shouting blood-curdling threats, 'or you'll be arrested for disturbing the peace.'

'But she's got my boy in there, my Ned,' protested Ma.

'Just grabbed the poor innocent child, she did,' said Cousin Annie. 'I wouldn't be surprised if she hasn't topped him by now.'

'We'll see about that,' said the policeman. And, marching up the steps, he unclipped the bullseye lantern from his belt and rapped sharply on the door with his wooden truncheon.

'Open up, in the name of the law!' he proclaimed in ringing tones.

'Who is it?' came a quavering voice from inside.

'Three members of the Greenwich Constabulary. Now open up or we shall be obliged to force our way in.'

The door opened a crack and Ruby peered round it, blinking in the bright light from the lantern.

'Don't cop me, officer,' she pleaded when she saw his top hat and long blue tunic. 'It wasn't my fault. I didn't want to do it. I told him I didn't want to. I said it was wrong to hurt a kid like that, specially such a little one, but he made me. He said we needed the money and . . .'

'Who exactly are we talking about, madam?' said the constable, waving his truncheon to stop her babbling. 'Who is "he"?'

'Me,' said a man. And Jake hobbled into the clearing leading a horse.

'And who are you, sir?' said the constable, lifting the lantern so he could see the man's face.

'I'm her husband.'

'I see. Well, since your wife appears to be a mite agitated, perhaps you'd be so good as to explain the situation.'

'Certainly, officer,' said Jake, putting on a most agreeable voice. 'I was woke up a short time ago by Jenny neighin'. I knew straight away somethin' was wrong so I opened the door and saw her gallopin' away and a boy standin' at my door gawpin' up at me. Thinkin' he was a thief, I told my missus to nab him while I went after the horse. Course, I realize now he wasn't no thief, the real one scarpered, but at least I got my horse back. She's a smart one,' he said, stroking her neck. 'Probably gave him a good kick and got away.'

Ma winced when she heard that but said nothing.

'Is this woman's son still with you?' The constable asked Ruby.

She nodded.

'Bring him out then.'

'She's got another kid, a girl, in there as well,' said Ma, as Ruby led out a badly shaken Ned. 'She's called Clara.'

'Not Clara Sterling?' The constable looked up sharply. 'Is that true?'

'Course it isn't. We wouldn't snatch a little kid, would we, Jake? We wouldn't do that, no matter how much they bribed us,' babbled Ruby, her face twisted in an expression of sheer terror. 'Not for a hundred, not for a thousand, not for —'

'She's lyin'!' shouted Ma. 'Look at her, you can

see she's tellin' whoppers. Ought to be in clink, she did.'

'Another word out of you and *you'll* be in clink,' growled the constable, waving his truncheon at her.

'Best place for her,' Jake said, glaring at Ma.

'I'll take a look in your caravan, sir, if I may,' said the constable.

'Do what you like.' Jake shrugged. 'You won't find no kid in there.'

'But Jem said . . .' began Cousin Annie. Ma gave her a warning look and she clamped her mouth shut. But it was too late.

'And who's Jem?' said the constable.

'My daughter Jem. That's short for Jemima,' said Ma. 'She said she thought Clara was in that caravan.'

'Oh, and what made her think that? Does she know her?'

'Nah, course she doesn't. Jem . . . I mean, Jemima's never clapped eyes on her.'

'You see, officer, they're only after the reward,' said Jake. 'They don't care about gettin' me and my missus into trouble, long as they get their hands on the ready.'

'It's true,' piped up Ruby. 'We're decent folk, we

are. We wouldn't help no one kidnap Clara Sterlin', even though her father's filthy rich and —'

'Shut your pan,' snapped Jake.

But the constable, who was not the most astute of men, ignored what Ruby was saying and turned his attention to Ma.

'What's your name?' he asked.

Ma stared at her feet and muttered something inaudible.

'Speak up, please.'

'I said, my name's Liza Perkins.'

'Perkins be blowed!' scoffed Jake. 'I'll wager she's lyin', officer. Sixpence says she's a Perkinski, same as the boy you're lookin' for.'

'Is that true?' said the constable.

Ma nodded. It would be easy enough for the police to find out her true name; her nosey neighbour at Devil's Acre, Ada Perry, would be delighted to tell them, if it meant getting her into trouble — and that's where she would be when they found out she had lied to them.

'Well, I'll be sniggered!' exclaimed Jake, slapping his thigh in delight. 'Looks as if you've found your villains, officer. And now maybe you'll leave innocent folk like me and my missus alone.'

'Come along, you,' said the constable, waving

his truncheon at Ma, Ned and Cousin Annie. 'I'm taking you in for questioning. And no funny business on the way, or we'll put the bracelets on you.'

38

Slithe carried Billy to a quiet glade in Greenwich Park, far from prying eyes, and dropping him on the ground, he took out his dagger.

'See this, do you?' he whispered, waving it close to the boy's eyes.

Billy nodded, too frightened to speak.

'You make a sound,' hissed Slithe, 'and I'll cut off your ears – like this.' He made a tiny nick in each of the boy's earlobes. 'You make a sound and I'll cut off your nose – like this.' With the tip of the dagger he made a tiny nick in the boy's nose. 'You make a sound and I'll cut off your —'

'I won't! I won't! I won't make a sound,' gasped Billy, his voice shaking with terror.

'Is this the boy, Slithe?' came a voice from the darkness at the edge of the glade.

Slithe spun round as if he had been struck. 'No. No, Master, it isn't,' he cringed. 'I was going to go after him, but this pesky varmint got in the way.'

'You fool!' The Master's voice was harsh as a whiplash, making Slithe cringe, his tongue darting in and out frenetically. 'You let Jem Perkinski escape?'

'Jem's my brother,' cried Billy — and instantly regretted it. 'I didn't mean it. I didn't mean to say nothin', guv,' he whimpered, cowering from Slithe.

'Leave him alone,' said the Master as Slithe raised his hand to strike Billy. 'Listen to me, boy. You say Jem Perkinski is your brother?'

'Yeh,' said Billy, peering into the gloom, but all he could make out was a shadow.

'And where is he now?'

'Don't know. He was pretendin' to nick the Pirate's horse but . . .'

'Why was he pretending?'

'So that the Pirate'd run after him and Ma and Cousin Annie could get in his caravan and nab that girl.'

'What girl?'

'Clara.'

Slithe began to snigger. 'Those stupid trollops thought the girl was in the caravan, Master. They don't know that she's —'

'Shut your mouth, you imbecile, or I'll send you back where you belong.'

'Sorry, sorry,' Slithe whined, writhing on the ground like a dog at the feet of a tyrannical master. 'There's something else.'

'What is it?'

'The woman — Ruby. She's scared. She started clacking to the police. She was going to squeal on us, Master.'

'Get rid of her.'

'Yes, Master. And the man?'

'Get rid of him too. We don't need them any more. They have served their purpose.'

'Yes, Master. Does that mean I'll get their share of the money?'

'If you do not find and destroy Jem Perkinski, Slithe, you will get no money at all.' The voice was icy. 'You will go back to the place from which I rescued you and there you will stay, rotting, for the rest of your days. Do I make myself clear?'

Slithe seemed to fold in on himself, burying his sleek head in the coils of his body. 'Yes, Master,' he whimpered. 'And what of the boy?' He pointed a scaly finger at Billy.

'He has seen you. He will incriminate you. Kill him. No . . . Wait, I have a better idea. Take him to Matilde and Paco. He will be useful to them on the

voyage back to Cadiz. Then they can tip him overboard.' The Master gave a sharp laugh. 'He will make a tasty snack for the Spanish sharks.'

39

The horse had gone one way and Jem the other. And when a man called, 'Jenny! Jenny!' with an answering neigh the horse had turned and trotted back to its master. In the distance Jem could hear shouts, his mother and Cousin Annie loudly protesting their innocence, and the stern rebukes of the police. It was obvious that his plan to rescue Clara had gone seriously awry and he waited till the hubbub had died down before making his way back.

He half feared Gran had been arrested as well, but to his relief the old woman was still there.

'Gran,' he whispered, creeping close to her, 'what's up?

But the old lady was so upset she could hardly speak. 'It's little Billy,' she managed to say at length. 'He's been nabbed.'

'*Nabbed?* Oh Lor', not him too.'

'I saw it, saw it with my own eyes, Jem. But there

was nothin' I could do. One minute he was there and the next . . .' She snapped her fingers.

'And what about Ma and Ned and Cousin Annie?'

'The crushers came and copped them. And all for nothin',' said the old woman bitterly, 'cos Clara wasn't in that poxy caravan. Nobody was, except the man with the wooden leg and a woman that kept caterwaulin' about she wasn't to blame.'

'Oh crimes!' said Jem, aghast at the bad news. 'Now what?'

'I'll see if these can help us,' said Gran. And reaching into her skirt she pulled out a bag.

'What've you got in there?'

The old woman said nothing. But stretching out her hands and throwing her head back she began to yowl in an eerie voice.

'What's wrong with you?' muttered Jem, staring at her in amazement. 'You got a pain in your tripes or somethin'?'

'Shh! I'm askin' the spirits to help me read the bones.'

'What bones?'

'Them.' And with a flourish the old woman opened the bag and tipped a pile of dry, bleached chicken bones on to the ground.

'Grub!' exclaimed Jem. And he picked up a bone and began gnawing it greedily.

'Put that down!' snapped Gran. 'That's your little brother Billy.'

'What?' Jem dropped it in horror. 'He's not . . . He's not dead, is he?'

'Nah, he's not. But that bone's him. And that one, the fat one by your foot, that's Cousin Annie. And the one next to it that's split in two,' she pointed at a wishbone, 'that's a married couple, Clara's mum and dad. And next to them is little Clara and . . . Lawks a mercy!' Gran put a hand over her mouth to muffle her cry of dismay.

'What's up? What can you see?' said Jem, leaning forward and peering at the bones intently.

'Get your block out the way,' said Gran, pushing him aside. 'Look at that one, all scaly and twisted,' she said, shuddering. 'He came out of that tree over there –' with a trembling finger she indicated a gnarled oak tree at the edge of the clearing – 'and wrapped himself round poor little Billy and took him away. Gone in a flash, he was, wormin' his way through the undergrowth.'

'I've seen him too, Gran. I'll wager he's the same one that nabbed Clara,' cried Jem, his voice rising in excitement. 'Where's he taken them? Ask the bones. Go on!'

Gran leaned forward, peering intently. 'Somewhere dark,' she said. 'Somewhere so small and hot and dark they can't hardly breathe in there.'

'In where?'

'Somewhere there's water.'

'What kind of water?'

'What d'you mean what kind of water? There's only one kind – wet.'

'But is it in a puddle or a barrel or a sewer or . . . ?'

'It's in the river.'

'What? That one?' said Jem, standing up and pointing to the Thames glinting like a long, silvery serpent in the light of the moon. 'Crikey, Gran. Pa says that one goes on for miles and miles. It stretches right round the world. Can't you ask them bones to be a bit more particular, like what part of the river, here or up at Westminster or . . .'

'They've told me all they're goin' to, son,' said Gran, picking them up and putting them back in the bag. 'Now it's up to us.'

40

Craddock could scarcely believe the evidence of his own eyes, but it certainly looked as if Mrs Sterling had stolen out of her house in the dead of night in order to meet someone in secret, an accomplice, a man to whom she was giving money. And for what? For having kidnapped her own daughter? It wasn't the first time a woman from the lower classes had married a rich man and tricked him out of his money, Craddock thought ruefully. But could he be wrong? He shook his head, trying to clear it of all extraneous thoughts. Was Mrs Sterling innocent? Was she herself being tricked by someone?

He was pondering this question when a light went on in the Sterlings' house. In an instant he was up the steps and hammering on their door.

Rose answered it in her night attire. 'Detective Inspector Craddock?' she said, looking at the detective in some amazement.

'I was just passing,' he said.

From the maid's incredulous expression, it was quite obvious she thought Craddock was either mad, drunk or a very bad liar.

'I was investigating a crime, a burglary, over there –' Craddock waved an arm vaguely in the direction of the houses on the other side of the square – 'and I saw the lights on here, so I . . .'

'Inspector Craddock. Come in, sir. Do come in,' said Mr Sterling, emerging from the drawing room. 'There has been a very disturbing development.'

'What has happened, sir?' said Craddock, as Mr Sterling showed him into the drawing room, where his wife sat weeping hysterically.

'Mrs Sterling could not sleep, which is understandable in the circumstances, so she went down to the kitchen with the intention of making herself some soothing drink when she saw a letter by the front door. Since it was addressed to me, she woke me – I confess I had finally managed to snatch a few moments of sleep – and when I read it —'

He was interrupted by a furious outbreak of sobbing from his wife, who cried, 'Clara! Oh, Clara!'

'It greatly distressed Mrs Sterling and she fainted,' he said, tenderly stroking her head in a vain attempt to calm her.

'So the letter had not been delivered before you retired for the night, sir?'

'Definitely not. I checked all the downstairs doors and windows before retiring, as is my custom.'

'May I see it?'

'Certainly.'

Mr Sterling drew the letter from his pocket and handed it to Craddock.

'"We want two thousand for the girl,"' Craddock read out loud. '"If you agree to pay up, put a pink carnation in your buttonhole and walk to work same way you used to then we'll let you know when and where to leave the ready don't tell the crushers or we'll deal with the kid."'

'"Deal with . . . ?" You see . . . ? You see . . . ? They're goin' to kill Clara!' shrieked Mrs Sterling.

Craddock looked at her askance. Either she was a devoted mother, genuinely distraught at the loss of her daughter, or she was a consummate actress who would soon, if all went according to her plan, get not only Clara back but also a great deal of money. And Mr Sterling? Craddock watched the elderly gentleman as he led his weeping wife from the room. She would abandon him, disappear without trace, probably to France or Italy, where no one would ever find her. She would have two thousand

pounds, while he, poor man, would be left alone and penniless.

'Mrs Restall is looking after her,' said Mr Sterling, coming back into the room. 'She is preparing her a sleeping draught of herbs.'

'Hmm . . .' Craddock reread the letter thoughtfully. 'Poor English. Clearly the sender is no scholar. Cheap paper. A second-rate nib.'

'You would surely not expect such a missive to come from a gentleman,' said Mr Sterling.

No, indeed, Craddock thought but didn't say. This is the work of one of your wife's friends in Seven Dials. Probably her lover. The two of them concocted this little ruse and most successful it might have been were it not for me, for I don't intend to let them get away with it.

'This warning,' he said out loud to Mr Sterling, *'"Don't tell the police or we'll deal with the girl . . ."'*

'Which I would most definitely have ignored, Inspector.'

'I congratulate you, sir. Many people bow to the demands of these scoundrels, which makes it difficult, if not impossible, for us to apprehend them.'

'What would you have me do now, inspector?'

'Where is your office?'

219

'Long Acre.'

'Then I suggest you walk to Long Acre with a pink carnation in your buttonhole. As soon as the rogues contact you again, inform Scotland Yard immediately. Does anyone, apart from Mrs Sterling, know of the contents of this letter?'

'No.'

'Then neither you nor Mrs Sterling must tell anyone that I was here tonight and saw it or . . .'

'Clara's life will be in danger. Yes, I understand perfectly, inspector.'

41

In the dead of night, when the darkness in the chain locker was so intense that Clara could not have seen her hand even if she had been able to hold it in front of her face, the hatch above was opened and something heavy – a sack, a bundle – was thrown on top of her.

'Ouch!' she cried out in pain, for whatever it was had stuck its elbow in her eye.

'Little present from Master,' said Matilde in a gloating voice. 'You look after, Clara.' And she slammed the hatch down and stomped away.

'Get off!' Clara raged as a knee went into her belly. 'Get off me!'

'I can't,' came the reply in a small voice. 'I can't move.'

'Roll on your side . . . Go on . . . Now I'll roll on mine . . . Careful where you put your feet . . . There, that's a bit better.'

'I can't hardly breathe.'

'Nor me. We'll just have to take it in turns.'

'I've got my arm stuck under your head and it hurts.'

'Well, pull it out . . . Nah, not my hair, you ninny!'

'Lor', your breath's horrible hot. It's burnin' me.'

'So's yours.'

'Where am I?'

'In a boat.'

'A boat? What, on water?'

'Where else, you goosecap. Who are you?'

'My name's Billy.'

'Billy what?'

'Billy Perkinski.'

'Lor', Billy, what're you doin' here?'

'D'you know me?'

'Course I do. I'm Clara Forbes — well, I was. We escaped from the Strand Workhouse together. Remember?'

'Clara!' cried Billy. 'Everyone's lookin' for you.'

'Are they? Are they really?'

'Well, Jem and Gran are.'

'What about my pa?'

'Don't know about him.'

'They want my pa to give them money to let me go.'

'Who's them?'

'The people on this boat.'

'And has he?'

'I don't know. I . . . I don't think so, else I wouldn't be here, would I?' said Clara in a small voice. And she began to cry, the tears running down her face and on to Billy's, as he was snuggled into her neck.

'What'll happen to you if your pa doesn't cough up?' he said.

'I don't know.'

'They're going to take me somewhere and tip me overboard so's I'm a tasty snack for Spanner sharks. What's a shark, Clara?'

'It's like a fish, a big fish, biggest fish you've ever seen,' said Clara, who had seen one in a book her father had given her, called *Wonders of the Deep*. 'When it opens its mouth you can see its teeth. Huge, they are, two rows of them, sharp as knives. When they sink them in you they rip you to bits.'

'Nah!' wailed Billy, his voice rising hysterically. 'Ma! I want my ma!'

42

In the early hours of the morning, after he had delivered a terrified Billy to the captain of *La Gaviota,* Slithe had doubled back to the glade where the old woman sat, muttering incoherently over a pile of bones. Winding his way up a tree, Slithe slid along an overhanging branch and stared at her and the girl in puzzlement. Although he ate any animal that crossed his path when he was hungry, be it a small dog, cat, rat or chicken, snapping its neck and tearing the flesh into pieces, he always threw the bones away. What use were they once he had torn off all the meat? And why, he wondered, did she put them into a bag and tuck them under her skirt as if they were jewels or gold coins?

Was she mad? The word made him snigger. Mad. That's what the warders in the lunatic asylum had called him. They had kept him in chains for as long as he could remember, since he was a boy, and when he had protested, driven even madder by the incessant cursing and roaring and screeching of the other inmates of Bedlam, the warders had whipped him and ducked him in a barrel of water, holding his head down until he nearly drowned.

But he had shown them . . . He chuckled, his thin lips drawn back over sharp, yellow teeth. He had shown them he was as sane as they were, as clever, as cunning as any man alive. For since the Master had freed him from Bedlam, had he not committed the most outrageous crimes? Had he not stolen the most beautiful jewels and gold and silver from the noblest families in the land? Had he not slit the throats of anyone who got in his way, as easily as killing a chicken? And he would go on doing so. As long as the Master told him to. There was nothing he would not do for him, no crime he would not commit. Without the Master's handsome bribes, a handful of guineas in the pocket of a greedy warder, another handful in the purse of a treacherous porter, he would still be in Bedlam, rotting in chains, his life slowly ebbing away in agony and despair. And this crime, the kidnapping of Clara Sterling, was the biggest, the best of all. The Master had planned it so carefully, every detail, and it had gone well — until some brat had spoilt it.

'Jem Perkinski!' He spat the name. 'Damn him! Damn him!'

The boy would blab, he'd tell the police, describe him to them – the scaly skin stretched tightly over the sleek, hairless head; the eyes, black, blank as a serpent's under their half-lids, the thin lips covering small, pointed teeth, sharp as daggers. The police would quickly put two and two together and realize the Snake they had been looking for for so long was the dangerous maniac who had escaped from Bedlam a year before. And then the Master, who had hidden him, sheltered him for so long would turn against him. He would throw him out, cast him on to the streets. And the police would capture him and take him back to the lunatic asylum, back to hell . . .

No, no, he had to find Jem Perkinski. He had to find him – and silence him.

He glanced down. The old lady and the girl had fallen asleep, their arms around each other. But Slithe did not sleep. He lay listening, watching, his beady eyes penetrating the darkness like a predatory reptile searching for its prey.

43

'I'm hungry!'

'Stop makin' that shindig, Billy,' Clara pleaded for the umpteenth time. 'It's no use; no one can hear you above the racket they're makin' out there and nobody cares neither. They just think you're some varminty little kid grizzlin' for nothin'.'

'But I'm hungry. I want some grub. I want a pork pie.'

'Well, you won't get one. All you'll get is a mouthful of gruel if you're lucky.'

'I don't like it here. It's dark,' whined Billy. 'I can't see nothin'.'

'That's cos there's nothin' to see. It's just a chain locker.'

'What's that?'

'It's where they store the chain when they've pulled up the anchor.'

'What's an anchor?'

Clara knew all about boats because her uncle

Bob had told her. Whenever he came ashore from his frigate she listened eagerly as he talked of tall masts that sometimes snapped in the gale-force winds, of billowing sails, the spanker, crossjack, jib, – of sailors crowded below deck in quarters so cramped they could barely turn over without squashing each other, of ship's biscuit as hard as nails and crawling with weevils, of the rum ration – a tot of rum a day to cheer up the men.

'When they want a boat to stop they can't pull on the reins like they do a horse,' Clara explained to Billy, 'so the sailors put somethin' real heavy, called an anchor, on the end of a long, thick chain and drop it to the bottom of the sea so's the boat can't move. The chain goes through a hole – it's called a hawse-hole, my uncle Bob says. You can't see it , but it's behind my shoulder.'

'And what happens when the sailors want the boat to go on? Do they say, "gee up"?' said Billy, who was getting rather confused with boats and horses.

'Course not, you goosecap. They pull on the chain, and the chain brings up the anchor.'

'And where does it go?'

'It hangs down the side of the boat and the chain . . .'

Billy waited.

'What about the chain, Clara?' he said when the girl still didn't go on.

'The chain comes in here.'

'But it can't. There's no room, cos we're in here.'

'The chain's stored here, Billy. When they pull up the anchor, that big, heavy chain's goin' to come in here and flatten us like the muffin man's pancakes.'

There was a moment's silence, then an ear-piercing scream.

'Ma! I want my ma!'

44

Jem woke with a start. Blinking, bleary-eyed, he stared into the darkness.

'Gran! Gran!' he whispered urgently, nudging her ribs with his elbow as Jake opened the door of his caravan and peered out. 'Look! Look! It's the Pirate! What's he doin'?'

'A moonlight flit, by the look of it,' said the old lady as Jake turned and beckoned to Ruby to follow him, crouching low as he crept down the steps, as if he feared someone would leap out.

'They're scared the crushers'll come back,' whispered Jem.

'So they should be. Anyone with half a brain can see they're up to no good,' said Gran.

Moving furtively, with many a backward glance, the couple untethered their horse and backed it into the shafts.

'I'll wager they know where Clara and Billy are. They'll lead us to them,' said Jem as the man swung

himself up into the driver's seat and with a soft, 'Get on, Jenny,' and a light flick of the whip urged the horse forward.

'You're right, Jem. We'll give them a minute or two so's they don't tumble we're followin' them, then we'll . . . Lawks a mercy, who's that?' Gran gasped as the dark shape of a man emerged from the trees and stole across the clearing after the caravan.

'Shh, Gran, or he'll hear you,' cautioned Jem, for there was something horribly sinister about the way the man was moving, slinking close to the ground, his sleek head weaving from side to side. But Jem's warning came too late. The man had heard them, for with a hissing sound he spun round and stared into the bushes where Jem and Gran were watching.

Jem squeezed his eyes tightly shut and scrunched into a ball. Beside him he heard his grandmother's trembling voice mumbling magic incantations, but she stopped as a blood-curdling scream rent the night air . . .

'Nah! Nah! Jake . . . he's got me! Help me, Jake!'

'Ruby, Ruby . . . Aargh!'

The man's voice gurgled into silence.

Then came the sound of doors opening, voices . . . Someone shrieked, 'Murder! Murder! Oh Lor', look what some fiend's done to them!'

'Come away . . . Quick!'

Doors slammed shut. Silence again.

With beating heart and bated breath Jem finally mustered up the courage to open his eyes and peer through the bushes. A ghastly scene greeted him. The caravan had come to a halt at the edge of the glade, the horse standing quietly in the shafts. Jake and Ruby had slumped to the ground, clutching each other in their death throes, their faces pale as ghosts in the moonlight.

'D-did he kill them, Jem?' whispered Gran. 'That man, did he kill the Pirate and his missus?'

Jem nodded. 'And he'll kill us too, cos he knows we saw him do it.'

'Lor', what was that?' Gran cried out as a twig snapped close by.

'It's him!'

'Run!'

'Nah, he'll get us. Hide!' said Jem, pulling Gran deeper into the undergrowth. 'We'll stay here till it's light and make a bolt for it . . . Gran, I saw his face — he's the one that nabbed Clara.'

'Yeh,' said the old woman grimly, 'he's the one that nabbed poor Billy too.'

There was a long silence as if Jem could hardly bring himself to say the terrible words, then he whispered, 'And I know who it is, Gran. He's the man that's done all them murders. I know it is cos he's got a face like a sna—'

'Stow it!' The old woman put a finger over his lips to stop him saying the dreaded name. 'I've never seen a face like it,' she said with a shudder, 'not even in my worst nightmares. And I hope I never see it again.'

'Gran, Cousin Annie said my name's on posters all over the fair. The crushers're lookin' for me cos I know what happened to Clara. That means . . .' Jem swallowed hard and started again, trying to keep the fear out of his voice. 'That means the Sna— that man — knows I saw him. He'll come after *me*, Gran. He'll try to stop me talkin'. He'll—'

'Shh, Jem,' Gran put her hand over his mouth. 'Keep quiet or he'll hear you.'

Coiled around the branch above their heads, Slithe watched the odd couple whispering together. He sensed their fear, smelled it. But he would not harm them, not yet, for he was sure that if he was patient, if he bided his time, they would lead him to the boy he was looking for. Sooner or later they would lead him to Jem Perkinski. And when they did . . .

He fingered the blade of his dagger, sticky now

with the blood of Jake and Ruby, and smiled. The Master would be pleased. He had done what the Master wanted. Now all he had to do was find Jem Perkinski. And kill him.

45

In the days when there were kings of Scotland, they lodged at the Palace of Whitehall when they visited London. Many years after the palace was burned down some pokey little houses were built on the land known as Great Scotland Yard adjacent to where the palace had once stood, and when the Metropolitan Police Force was formed it converted one of these houses into its headquarters.

Anyone visiting this building might justifiably have expected to find it a model of working efficiency, with a place for everything and everything in its place. The reverse was true. Scotland Yard, as it came to be known, bore a striking resemblance to a jumble sale, with piles of books, clothes, blankets and tack piled in every conceivable and sometimes inconceivable place. But Detective Inspector Craddock had other things on his mind than his shambolic surroundings as he mounted the stairs, stepping over a pile of discarded uniforms in order to get into his office, for he had a request to make of his superintendent.

'What's his mood, Jenkins?' he asked his sergeant.

'To put it bluntly, sir, I reckon he must've got out of bed the wrong side this morning. Again.'

Craddock's heart sank. He knew he had over-stepped the mark by involving himself in Clara's kidnapping, and if Superintendent Hamilton-Harley was to find out he'd poked his nose in without his authority there would be hell to pay. The solution was to persuade Hamilton-Harley to appoint him investigating officer on the case, but that would not be easy, as he well knew.

'I gave you a day off so you could rest, man,' the superintendent grumbled, 'not for you to go chasing all over Greenwich fair after a missing girl.'

'But, sir . . .'

'I simply cannot afford to release you now, Craddock. The gentlemen of the press – gentlemen, bah! – are hounding us day and night, demanding to know when we're going to catch the Snake. They're beginning to call us incompetent – the impertinence of it! – although I have explained on many occasions that we have no clues, no clues whatsoever. The wretched man always seems to slip out of our grasp like a . . . like a . . .'

'Snake?' suggested Craddock.

'Precisely. I'll put Detective Inspector Mullins on the kidnap case.'

'But, sir, I have a hunch . . .'

As soon as he had said it Craddock knew he had made a mistake. Although he had solved many a crime with what he called 'a feeling in my bones', it was unwise to admit it to a military man.

Hamilton-Harley's face turned a rusty shade of red and his jowls wobbled in fury. 'We do not work on hunches in the police force,' he barked.

'I beg your pardon, sir. All I meant was, given sufficient time I am confident I can bring these kidnappers to justice. I have my . . .' Craddock hesitated, searching for a word that would not antagonize the superintendent further, 'suspicions. And I fear that if Mr Sterling pays the ransom money the criminals will get away scot-free. I don't need to tell you that we shall then have similar kidnappings all over the country and the press will be down on us like a ton of bricks. We need to stop this now, sir, nip it in the bud before it spreads like a rash.'

'That is a mixed metaphor,' growled Hamilton-Harley.

'I beg your pardon, sir.' Craddock tried hard to

keep his face straight, for his commanding officer was a stickler for form, in thought, word and deed. 'My grammar has never been very good, especially early in the morning.'

Superintendent Hamilton-Harley leaned back, tugging thoughtfully at his waxed moustache. He was loath to take Craddock off a case that was causing the police so much aggravation, but was forced to admit that they were making no headway with it; the scent had grown cold, the Snake had seemingly gone to ground. The criticism from the press and general public was getting louder by the day, but the kidnapping of the daughter of a middle-class gentleman would take their minds off the Snake and her recovery would restore Scotland Yard's credibility. If anyone could do it, he thought, Craddock could.

'I shall have to clear it, of course,' he harrumphed.

'Thank you, sir.'

It was only a formality and both of them knew it. Just as Craddock always got his man, Hamilton-Harley always got his way.

'Jenkins!' Craddock shouted, hurrying back to his office. 'Jenkins!'

'You wanted me, sir?' said the sergeant, appearing in the doorway with a mug of tea in his hand.

'I have a job for you, sergeant. I want you to go to Victoria Square and keep a discreet lookout.'

'And who or what am I looking out for, sir?'

'The accomplice of a treacherous woman.'

46

Mr Sterling's offer of a reward did indeed 'loosen someone's tongue', as Craddock had hoped. Unfortunately it loosened too many. No sooner had the notices been posted in strategic positions throughout the fairground and Greenwich Park than the local police station was inundated with men and women, all of them convinced they knew the whereabouts of a little girl answering the description of Clara Sterling. They had seen her in every booth, behind every stall, on every stage, in every cart, under every table. And worse, far worse for the beleaguered constable on the desk at Greenwich police station, were the hundreds who had dragged some unfortunate boy in by the collar.

It mattered not a jot that the boy bore no resemblance whatsoever to Jem Perkinski. As long as he was within about five years or so of Jem's age and in possession of two arms and two legs, the poor wretch could have had black, brown or blond hair;

blue, green or grey eyes; round, square or pointed ears; a full set of teeth or none; spots or no spots . . .

'Here's your villain, officer. Here's the wretch that nabbed that poor little girl,' the boy's captor would cry, thrusting him under the constable's nose. 'Give me the money, guv.'

The constable raised his eyes to the heavens in despair. At this rate, he thought, every boy in the fair would sooner or later be dragged along for his inspection. To make it worse, he was beginning to think that he'd seen some of them before. That one with the ginger curls and snub nose, he'd definitely seen him twice, if not three times.

'But, Mum, I didn't do it. I didn't nab that girl,' protested the freckle-faced lad.

'I know that, you ninny,' snapped his mother, 'but I'll get a hundred pounds for you. That's more than I'll earn in my whole life, so shut your trap.'

At one point a fight broke out between three or four men, all claiming that their boy was Jem Perkinski. Within seconds everyone else had joined in and there was so much punching, kicking and hair-pulling that the constable put on his steel-plated helmet and dived under the desk, muttering, 'I'm tempted to go lookin' for that pesky kid and get the reward for myself.'

47

When he married, Mr Sterling had stopped walking to and from his work so that he could spend more time with his family, but on that fine spring morning he did as Inspector Craddock had instructed and strode out, a pink carnation that Mrs Restall had picked from the garden prominently displayed in his buttonhole, past Buckingham Palace, across Green Park, along Piccadilly and through Leicester Square to Long Acre.

Although his stomach was in knots, he tried to appear as calm as he could. Nevertheless as he went he searched every face, trying to tell by a scowl, the flicker of a smile or the twitch of an eyelid if that dapper young bank clerk in his black frock coat and tall chimney-pot hat or that lady's maid in her long skirts and shawl had sent him the ransom letter.

Over the years he had built up a nodding acquaintance with many people on his route, and they all greeted him warmly.

'I see you're back to Shanks's pony, guv,' chortled a screever, looking up from the portrait of Prince Albert he was chalking on the pavement. 'Better for the health, eh, than going by carriage?'

'"Shank's pony"?' Mr Sterling frowned. What did it mean? Was it a coded message? '"Better for the health"?' Why had the man said that? Was there some sinister meaning behind it?

'Nice to see you again, sir,' said a flower seller. 'You don't need none of my blooms, though,' she laughed, pointing at the carnation in his buttonhole. 'More's the pity.'

Mr Sterling stepped back in alarm. Was the woman trying to tell him something?

'What's wrong, sir?' she said, the laughter dying on her lips. 'If I said somethin' out of place, I apologize. I was only jokin'.'

'No, no, it's nothing,' said Mr Sterling, hurrying on.

'What's wrong with him?' she muttered to one of the crossing sweepers when he'd gone. 'He used to be such a civil gen'leman. Always had a kind word and a smile.'

'Marriage,' retorted the sweeper with a knowing grimace. 'I've seen it happen hundreds of times. Soon as a man gets a wife and kids he stops smilin'.'

 243

'Nah, I think it's worse than that,' said the flower seller, watching Mr Sterling as he walked up the street, his head swivelling from left to right, 'I'd say he was scared.'

No sooner had Mr Sterling arrived at his office, a small but elegantly furnished room above the coachworks, than there was a knock on the door and in answer to his, 'Pray, come in,' Septimus Mallick entered.

He was a very tall, slightly built man some twenty years younger than his senior partner, his dark hair parted in the middle and kept in place with a liberal application of bear's grease, his eyes deep set under straight eyebrows. Like most Victorian men his crowning glory was his facial hair, a generous growth that covered the space between his ears, cheekbones and chin, similarly restrained with bear's grease.

'My dear sir,' he hurried forward, putting both hands on Mr Sterling's desk and leaning towards him urgently. 'What news of Clara?'

'Nothing as yet, I regret,' said Mr Sterling.

Mallick sank into a chair and closed his eyes in anguish. 'I have been up all night, my mind in turmoil. It was all I could do not to return to the fair

244

to continue the search for her but my mother advised against it. She said I should leave it to the police, who are far more capable than I of tracking down villains.'

'That good lady is quite right, Septimus,' agreed Mr Sterling, 'although I too felt a great desire to return to the fair. But where would I look?' He raised his hands despairingly. 'Clara might be many miles away by now. She might even be . . .' His voice faltered.

'Don't! Don't say it, Mr Sterling. Do not even think it.' Mallick shot to his feet, clearly agitated. 'Has there been nothing, not the slightest indication of Clara's whereabouts?'

Now Mr Sterling was in a quandary. He had given his word to Inspector Craddock that he would not tell anyone about the ransom letter, but Mallick had been his partner for many years and he knew him to be an utterly trustworthy man. And Mallick was so obviously distraught at the loss of little Clara it seemed unkind not to share with him this latest piece of hopefully good news.

'There has been a communication, a letter,' said Mr Sterling, taking it from an inner pocket and handing it to the young man.

When he had read it Mallick's eyes lit up. 'But

this is wonderful, sir, quite wonderful. All you have to do is pay the sum of money and dear little Clara will be . . . Why, what is wrong?' He frowned, for Mr Sterling looked more distressed than ever.

'The money,' he murmured. 'Two thousand pounds.'

'It is an outrageous amount, I agree. But for Clara, surely . . . ?'

'For Clara I would give anything. But I will be frank with you, Septimus. For the past twenty years I have been running two establishments: my own house in Victoria Square and one in Finchley which I purchased for my brother, who is an invalid, and his two daughters, unmarried ladies of a certain age who are unable to support themselves. I have never regretted it, but it has placed a heavy financial burden on me. Even if I were to sell my own home and move into a more modest residence in a less salubrious area, I could not hope to raise two thousand pounds . . . and in any case, the money is needed immediately. I tell you, Septimus, I am at my wits' end,' he concluded, wringing his hands as if to wrench them off his wrists.

Mallick began to pace up and down the room, his brow puckered in thought.

'The banks, sir. Surely they would give you a loan?'

'Indeed they would. But at such a great rate of interest, since I am an elderly gentleman, that I could never hope to repay it.'

'And you have no relatives, no friends who could help you?'

'No relatives other than the three who are entirely dependent on me. As for my friends, they are comfortably off. But two thousand pounds . . .' Mr Sterling's voice trailed away.

Septimus Mallick continued to walk up and down, frowning and muttering under his breath as if he were engaged in an argument with himself. Abruptly he stopped, his mind seemingly made up, leaned on Mr Sterling's desk again and said, 'If you were willing to sell this company, sir, I would be willing to buy it. At this very moment. For two thousand pounds.'

Mr Sterling opened his mouth to say something but he was so surprised, nothing came out.

'As you know,' continued Mallick, 'I recently received a substantial legacy from my aunt. I will give it to you in its entirety if you will give me the deeds of Sterling & Mallick Ltd. I hasten to add that you are most welcome to continue in my employ for as long as you wish. What do you say, sir?'

Mr Sterling reached out, his eyes shining, and grasped Mallick's hand. 'That is most generous — a most generous offer, Septimus,' he said.

'Then it is settled,' said Mallick, giving Mr Sterling's hand a hearty shake. 'I shall go to the banks straight away and withdraw the money. You shall have it within the hour and, God willing, Clara will soon be home safe and sound. There is just one thing.'

'And what is that?'

'Despite what is said in that wretched letter I strongly urge you to show it to the police.'

'In truth, Septimus, I have already done so. But I promised Inspector Craddock that I would not tell anyone.'

'And nor, sir, shall I,' said Mallick solemnly. 'You have my word upon it.'

48

Jem and Gran waited till the sun was well up and the fairground beginning to fill with people before making their move. Slithe, who had spent the dark hours watching them, hidden among the branches of an ancient elm, emptied the dregs of a gin bottle down his scaly throat and slithered closer to hear what they were saying. 'Kate.' Several times he heard them say the name. Who was Kate?

When they set off he followed them, staying close to the ground, slithering through the under-growth. Down the hill they went and across the greensward towards the fairground, looking over their shoulders every other minute, the old woman hobbling, complaining that she was stiff and her feet hurt and she couldn't go so fast, the other one strid-ing out . . . Such an ungainly girl, Slithe thought, watching her with distaste. She kept tripping over her skirt, tugging at her bodice, pushing her bonnet back up, wiping her nose on her sleeve.

Through the fairground they hurried until they reached the dancing booth. A girl was sitting on the ground by the entrance, her expression glum. Slithe slithered up the side of the booth and across the top, to look down on the scene below. Though he caught very little of their conversation it was obvious to him that this girl was the Kate they had spoken of and that she was upset . . .

'Somethin' awful's happened,' Kate said to Gran. 'Me, Shep and 'Enry were in there, singin' and dancin' all night.' She nodded at the dancing booth, quiet now, the waiters and musicians asleep under the tables. 'When they kicked us out we dossed down here. I put the ready I'd taken for all your bottles of muck – I mean, your bottles of Miracle of Life – in the purse under my skirt, but when I woke up it'd gone. And so had 'Enry and Shep.'

'They took my money?'

'Not 'Enry. He wouldn't do nothin' like that. But Shep . . .' Kate pulled a face.

'Lawks a mercy, things're goin' from bad to worse for us Perkinskis,' moaned Gran.

'Why? What's happened?' said Kate.

'Billy's been nabbed,' said Jem.

Kate, who had been ignoring him until then,

gave Jem a hard look. 'Who's she, Gran? Your *new* helper?' she said in an aggrieved voice.

'Nah.' Gran leaned forward and whispered in her ear, 'It's Jem . . . shh!' She put a hand over Kate's mouth before she could cry out. 'He's dressed like a girl cos the crushers are after him.'

'The crushers are always after him,' said Kate.

'But this time it's serious,' said Gran grimly. 'Real serious.'

'And there's worse,' said Jem.

'*Worse?*' Kate echoed incredulously.

'We saw the man who's been killin' all them people.'

'Nah!' Kate turned deathly white. 'You don't mean . . . ? You can't mean . . . ? Not the Sna—?'

'Yeh, him,' said Jem quickly.

'You *saw* him?'

'Yeh.'

'Where?'

'Here at the fair. He killed two people. We saw him do it.'

'Oh Lor'!' Kate clutched her throat.

'So now he'll be after me too.'

'Oh Lor', we'd best find Ma and Pa and . . .'

'Nah, your pa's in hospital,' said Gran, 'and your

251

ma and aunts and uncles and Ned've all been copped by the crushers.'

'Oh Lor'!' cried Kate. 'Oh Lor'!'

49

When Septimus Mallick had gone, Mr Sterling sat for a long time, his eyes closed, his head in his hands, pondering the strange turn his life had taken. In the past year he had acquired a wife and two children but had lost his company, a company he had established as a young man and worked diligently to make a success. But what else could he do? he thought, sighing deeply. He needed the money to pay Clara's ransom and it was his great good fortune that Mallick was prepared to let him have it. Two thousand pounds, a prodigious sum. Mr Sterling shook his head in disbelief. He had had no idea that Mallick's aunt had left him such a fortune. With wise management of his finances, the young man could have ceased working and led a life of relative ease. But he was fiercely ambitious, too full of energy to waste his time wafting from one dinner party to the next . . . No, Mr Sterling had no doubt that his erstwhile partner wanted to make his mark on the world, and what better way to do it than take control of Sterling & Mallick Ltd – soon to be just Mallick Ltd?

But what of me? Mr Sterling thought. What shall I do now? Mallick had said he could stay, but in what capacity? No longer as a senior partner, nor even a junior one. He would be no more than Mallick's employee, a clerk, one of the dozen or so sitting in the outer office at that very moment, bent over their desks, a quill pen in hand, writing orders and receipts in immaculate copperplate.

Ah well, he managed a smile, albeit a wry one; whatever he did it would bring in a small income for as long as he had the strength to work. And though he would have to give up his home in Victoria Square for something much more modest, he would get his beloved Clara back. They would be a family again.

There was a knock on the door and, without waiting for an answer, Septimus Mallick came in carrying a case.

'There, Charles,' he said, putting it on the table. 'Two thousand pounds in various denominations from twenty to a hundred. Unfortunately the bank had no thousand-pound notes, which would have

made it so much easier to carry,' he added, opening the lid of the case.

'Two thousand,' murmured Mr Sterling, reaching out to touch the notes. 'What will they do with it all, I wonder?'

'Lose it, I hope, or, better still, have it stolen from them, which is what they deserve,' said Mallick angrily.

'It is extraordinarily kind of you to help me in this way, but how am I to get the money to Clara's kidnappers?'

'You have heard nothing from them since receiving the letter?'

'Nothing.'

'Then, Charles, all you can do is wait.'

'And that, sir,' said Mr Sterling despairingly, 'is the hardest part of all.'

50

By the time Jem and Gran had told her all about the kidnapping of Clara and then Billy, Kate was very frightened indeed.

'We should go home,' she cried. 'It isn't safe here. He'll kill us. That man. He'll . . .'

'We can't go.' Gran stopped her with a stern look. 'We've got to find Billy and we've got to find Clara as well as clearing Jem's name.'

'And where're you goin' to look for them?' snapped Kate, her voice rising shrilly. 'You don't have no idea where they are, no idea at all. Lookin' for two little kids in this lot –' with a sweep of her hand she indicated the vast crowds now thronging the fairground – 'is like lookin' for a noodle in a haystack. If you ask me, Jem, you should go to the crushers and tell them what you saw.'

'The crushers? Me go to the crushers?' Jem could scarcely believe his ears. No Perkinski ever went to

the police, and certainly not to help them. 'I'd sooner cut my throat,' he said.

'Someone else'll do it for you soon enough if you don't,' retorted Kate. 'My throat too. And Gran's. And . . . Now what?' She frowned as Shep came running up, his arms full of oranges, followed by Henry, haranguing him vigorously.

'Oh crimes, don't keep on about it,' Shep shouted back. 'It's only a few pesky oranges.'

'But they're not ours,' Henry ranted at him. 'It doesn't matter if it's only a few. You stole them.'

'But they won't know. They've got loads.'

'Shep, for Lor's sake!'

'And where's my money?' cried Kate, venting all her frustration on Shep.

'My money, you mean,' growled Gran.

'What money? I don't know what you're talkin' about. I haven't got none. Look,' Shep said, throwing the oranges on the ground and turning his pockets inside out to show they were empty. 'Someone else must've taken it.'

'You nabbed it, Shep. You did. You must've,' insisted Kate.

'I keep tellin' you I didn't. All I done is nabbed – I mean, borrowed – a few oranges.'

 257

Slithe watched the scene below, his eyes, black as night, darting from one face to the other. He had been excited when the two boys came running up, but his high hopes quickly turned to disappointment, for neither of them fitted the description he'd been given of Jem Perkinski. The boy he was after was much younger than these two, much shorter, stockier, more like the girl, not the redhead shrieking and waving her arms about, but the other one, the one who had come with the old woman. She was talking now, asking one of the boys a question. Slithe inched forward, straining to hear, but the raucous noise of the fairground muffled their voices and he writhed in frustration.

'Where d'you get them oranges?' asked Jem.

'What's it to you, my poppet?' said Shep, giving him a chuck under the chin.

'She's my sister,' said Kate, before Jem could flare up. 'Her name's . . . er . . .'

'Jemima,' said Gran.

'*Jemima*. That's a tall name for a short girl.' Shep grinned. 'But she's a nice piece of goods,' he said, running his eye over Jem admiringly.

Jem was about to give him a punch on the nose but decided it would be unwise in the circum-

stances. Restraining himself with difficulty he growled, 'I said, where d'you get them oranges?'

'Well, *Jemima*, it's none of your business, my ducky, but I'll tell you anyway. The fact is, me and Henry've been up since five wherryin' people to the fair, and by the time we got back here with a boatload we were hungry and in need of a bite to eat.'

'We could've bought some grub,' Henry interrupted him. 'We'd got the ready.'

'But that's sappy, isn't it? Why spend the ready when there was one of them Spanish schooners so full of oranges it was practically sinkin' in the water? Why buy an orange when there're plenty just askin' to be taken?'

'They weren't askin',' growled Henry. 'There just happened to be a pile of them on deck for the crew.'

'So I thought, oranges make a tasty breakfast, I thought,' said Shep, ignoring him. 'Lucky there was no one around; they were all sleepin' below, except for a kid that kept bawlin', "Ma. I want my ma."'

Jem frowned. 'I thought you said it was a Spanish ship.'

'It was.'

'You know Spanish, do you?' said Jem, who'd heard the Spanish onion sellers in the market talking to each other.

'Nah, course not,' retorted Shep, looking rattled.

'Then how'd you know what the kid said?'

'Cos he said it in English, that's why. And – this'll make you laugh – he kept squealin', "I'm hungry! I'm hungry!"' Shep imitated the plaintive cry of a small child. '"I want a pork pie."'

51

At dawn the river had come to life. Scrunched in the tiny chain locker with Billy pressed so hard against her it made her ribs ache, Clara could hear the sounds of boats arriving while others prepared to leave, and above all the clanking and grinding were the screams of seagulls and the shouts of the river folk, the sailors, fishermen and mudlarks.

Billy, who had slept fitfully, woke up and began crying again. 'It's so dark in here. And it's hot. And I can't move. And what's that noise? Clara . . .' he dug his elbow in her bruised ribs, 'what's that noise?'

'I think . . .' Clara faltered. 'I think they're gettin' ready to move, Billy.'

'We're goin'?'

'Yeh.'

'Are they pullin' up the anchor?'

'Yeh.'

'And that big chain will come in here and squash us?'

261

'Yeh.'

Billy began to sob. 'Don't want to die. I want my ma! Ma! I want my ma!'

The hatch to the locker was opened abruptly and Matilde stood glaring down at them. Clara had difficulty seeing her after so many hours in darkness, and she blinked blindly in the sunlight.

'Stop you noise!' snapped the woman. 'Get out! Come! Fast! Fast!' she said, yanking the two children up with strong arms.

'You be there,' she said, pushing them on to the deck. 'You be quiet, say nothing, or I . . .' She made a slicing motion across her neck.

Before Clara had accustomed herself to the brightness sufficiently to look about her, she and Billy were covered with a heavy tarpaulin, stinking of tar.

'What's happenin', Clara?' whispered Billy, snuggling into her.

Clara heard the chain screeching as the anchor was slowly pulled in, the crew barking commands to each other in Spanish, and then she felt the boat shudder. Many times her uncle Bob had described the moment when the wind filled its sails and a boat sprang to life. Thrilling, he'd said it was, exhilarating, like seeing a wild animal let out of a cage and running free.

Clara's eyes filled with tears. She would never run free again. She would never see her mother or father or Pip . . .

'What's happenin', Clara?' persisted Billy.

'We're goin',' she said, feeling the boat surge forward.

'Where?'

'I reckon we're goin' to Spain. That's where this lot come from.'

'Where's Pain?'

'A long way from here. The other side of the world.'

'And do they eat there?'

'Course they do.'

'What do they eat?'

'They eat . . . er . . . oranges and . . . er . . .'

'Pork pies? Do they eat pork pies?'

'Nah – I mean, no, I don't think they have pork pies in Spain. They only have oranges.'

'Don't want no oranges,' whimpered Billy. 'Don't want to go to Pain. I want a pork pie. Want a pork pie!'

'¡Basta!' growled Matilde, giving the tarpaulin a hard kick with the toe of her boot. 'Enough!'

52

'A pork pie?' Jem gasped. 'You said the kid on that Spanish boat was hollerin' for a pork pie?'

'That's right.' Shep nodded. 'The little varmint wouldn't shut up.'

'Crikey, it must be Billy!'

'Who's Billy?'

'My brother.'

'Oh yeh? What's your brother doin' on a Spanish boat?'

'That's what I'd like to know,' said Jem grimly. 'Where is it?'

'Moored about a hundred yards from the jetty.'

'Could we get on it?'

'We could get up close.'

'All right, let's go,' said Jem. 'We can use Henry's boat.'

'My boat,' interjected Shep. 'It's half mine.'

'It's *my dad's* boat, Shep,' said Henry. 'He only lent it to us till we can buy one of our own.'

Shep scowled. 'So he won't want us messin' about lookin' for some pesky brat, will he? We've got a job of work to do. We've got to make some money.'

'Nah. I'm goin' to help look for Billy, Shep.'

'Well, I'm off. I can row the boat without you. And all the money I make'll be mine.'

'You're not takin' that boat nowhere,' said Henry, squaring up to him.

'Huh! And who's goin' to stop me?'

'I am.'

Now Shep was stronger than Henry, but Henry had taken boxing lessons from Ben Caunt, the landlord of the Coach and Horses in St Martin's Lane, one of the most famous bare-knuckle prize fighters in the country. Henry, although a gentle boy at heart, had learned to box in order to defend himself in the rough world in which he was forced to live. He was as light on his feet, agile and quick-witted as Shep was slow and lumbering. And Shep knew in any contest he would be the loser.

'You can keep your poxy boat,' he growled. 'I hope it sinks – and you lot with it.'

And feigning indifference, he walked off with a jaunty swagger.

53

'There's a boy downstairs, sir,' said a sergeant, appearing in the doorway of Craddock's office. 'Says he's got something important for you. Says he was told to give it to you and no one else.'

'Very well, sergeant, show him up.'

'He won't come up, sir. Says if you want it you can come and get it! I was tempted to cuff his ear and send him on his way, but I managed to restrain myself, sir, just in case he really does have something important for you.'

'Oh, all right, I'll come down,' sighed Craddock.

A small, scruffy boy was waiting by the entrance door. 'Your name Craddock, guv?' he asked when the inspector went over to him.

'It is.'

'A bloke told me to give you this.'

He held up a sealed letter, but when Craddock reached out to take it the urchin thrust it behind his

back and said, 'The old fogey said as how you'd give me twopence for it.' And he held out his hand.

'Are you sure it's for me?' said Craddock suspiciously.

'That your name?' said the boy, holding up the letter.

Craddock bent forward to read it. 'Yes.'

'Then it must be for you, mustn't it?'

Somewhat irritated by the boy's cocky attitude, Craddock nevertheless handed over the required twopence and breaking the seal read the brief message inside – '*I have received a further communication. Meet me at St Margaret's.*' It was signed 'Charles Sterling'.

Pocketing the letter, Craddock put on his top hat and strode down Whitehall and across Parliament Square. There were a dozen or more people in St Margaret's, some with their heads bowed in prayer, others lost in thought or gazing at the stained-glass window above the altar. Mr Sterling was sitting at the end of a pew, seemingly engrossed in *The Book of Common Prayer*.

Craddock took a place in a pew in the back row, from where he had a good view of the church. Leaning forward, he covered his face with his hands as if praying and peered through his fingers. Nobody appeared to be paying any attention to him or to

 267

Mr Sterling. He sat back and glanced around, pretending to admire the statues and paintings. As far as he could tell, there was nobody hidden behind columns or in dark corners.

Out of the corner of his eye he saw Mr Sterling close the prayer book, put it on the seat next to him, get up and wander along the side aisle. Craddock counted to twenty and then he too got up and ambled in an apparently aimless way to where Mr Sterling had been sitting. Checking again that he wasn't being watched, Craddock sat down and picked up the prayer book. A letter had been hidden between the cover and the front page.

A priest came out of the vestry. Craddock waited as the man crossed before the altar, stopping to genuflect, and left by a side door, before he opened the letter and read, 'Go to the Fresh Wharf and you'll see an empty rowing boat floating downstream put the ready in it and go home. If you tell the crushers we'll get the ready but you won't never get the kid back you have been warned.'

Mr Sterling had stopped in front of a sarcophagus and appeared to be admiring it, bending forward to read the Latin inscription. Craddock pocketed the letter and walked slowly up the aisle until he was alongside Mr Sterling, who turned and with

a half-smile and a nod of the head pointed to the inscription as if he was asking Craddock for a translation.

'Forgive my curt invitation, inspector, and the rather unorthodox method of delivering it,' he whispered, 'but since I am obviously being followed I thought it wiser to meet you here than go to Scotland Yard. Many people might consider it disrespectful to use a church as a place of assignation, but I am convinced that God will understand and forgive.'

'I am sure you are right, sir,' murmured Craddock. 'This letter is in the same rough hand as the first. Who delivered it to you?'

'I don't know, inspector. I went to the chapel of ease, and when I returned to my office the letter was on my desk. I thought it wiser to come straight here than waste time questioning my employees . . . I mean, my former employees.'

'Former?'

'The company no longer belongs to me. My junior partner has purchased it. I have the ransom money here. I thought—'

'*Hic jacet* . . .' Craddock interrupted him in a louder voice as a woman at the front of the church got up and walked past them. 'If my memory serves

me well, sir — and I confess it is some years since I studied the Latin language, that means . . .' He glanced over his shoulder, making sure the woman had gone. 'You say you have the ransom money with you?'

'Here, in this case, inspector,' said Mr Sterling, patting it.

'Then we must hasten to the Fresh Wharf,' said Craddock. 'You, sir, will go by hansom cab. When you get there, employ the services of a waterman to row you to the middle of the river. When you see the empty boat, put the money in it and return instantly.'

'To the dock?'

'To your home, sir. The kidnappers must see that you are obeying their instructions to the letter.'

'Not quite to the letter, inspector.'

'What do you mean?'

'Let me explain . . .'

54

'Come on, plaguy quick,' said Henry, running through the fair, 'before that Spanish boat sets sail.' But they had hardly gone ten yards when a huge, thuggish-looking man pounced on Kate, pinning her arms behind her back and bellowing, 'What's your name, eh? Come on, spit it out.'

'K-Kate,' stammered the frightened girl.

'Let her alone,' cried Henry, running up to defend her.

'What about that one?' said the man, releasing Kate and making a lunge at Jem. 'Her name Clara, is it?'

'Course it isn't, Rog,' said a second man, coming up behind him. 'This one's a redhead and the other one's dark. The girl we're lookin' for is blonde. 'Sides, she's much younger than these two.'

'Yeh, you're right. Drat! That pesky kid's got to be somewhere. A hundred quid! A hundred quid for findin' her . . . And I'm goin' to, if it's the last thing

I do,' said the man called Rog, striding off with a determined expression, followed by his companion.

'A hundred quid,' said Henry when they'd gone.

'A hundred . . . Blimey!' echoed Jem.

'It's a tidy sum,' said Gran.

'And if we find Clara . . .'

'We'll get it.'

'D'you reckon she's on that boat?'

'I reckon Billy is.'

'And if he's there . . .'

'There's a good chance she'll be too.'

'Right, let's go.'

'Nah, we can't,' said Henry.

'Why not?'

'Cos I can't row us all without Shep.'

'I can row,' said Jem.

Henry looked at him askance. 'A girl? Row?' he said in disbelief.

'He isn't a girl,' Kate whispered in his ear. 'He's my brother Jem in disguise cos he's hidin' from the crushers. But don't believe him – he can't row.'

'I can,' said Jem hotly.

'You've never been in a boat in your life.'

'Course I have. I've been in dozens, hundreds. I can row anythin'.'

'Oh yeh?'

'See that.' He pointed to a steamer plying its way downriver. 'I've rowed one of them.'

'Don't be a ninny,' said Henry. 'Them boats don't have oars. They've got engines.'

Jem turned a pretty shade of pink. 'Yeh . . . Well . . . I used to row one,' he blustered, glaring at Kate, who was laughing so much she had to hold her sides, 'before it got an engine.'

Slithe was puzzled. Where were they going now, all of them, hurrying towards the river as if their lives depended on it?

He let out a long hiss of exasperation, slithered down the side of the tent and followed them at a discreet distance, keeping his head well down and his eyes on the ground lest other, prying eyes should see him.

55

Sergeant Jenkins hid his bulky form in some bushes from where he had a good view of the Sterlings' house.

'Watch out for a man loitering in the square,' Craddock had instructed him. 'If Mrs Sterling leaves the house, follow her. If she meets up with a man, arrest them both and bring them in for questioning.'

'May I ask why, sir?' Jenkins had asked.

'Prepare yourself for a shock.'

'I've been in this job many years, sir. I've heard everything and I've seen everything. Nothing shocks me any more.'

'It is my belief that Mrs Sterling arranged for Clara to be kidnapped.'

'Well, blow me down!' Jenkins had exclaimed, clearly shocked.

'I think she paid a person or persons to snatch the girl.'

'So she's blackmailing her own husband?'

'That would appear to be the case.'

'What a hussy.'

'Indeed.'

'Does he know?'

'Not as yet.'

'It'll break his heart, poor man.'

Jenkins was considering the perfidy of women as he took up his position in Victoria Square. Who, he wondered, was Mrs Sterling's partner in crime, the man Craddock had seen taking money from her?

Apart from a tramp curled up under a tree fast asleep, there were few people in sight that fine spring morning. The milkman came down the street leading a cow, and Maisie, the Sterlings' maid, ran up the area steps from the kitchen with a large jug. Jenkins watched as the man milked the cow into the jug, took some coins from the maid and walked on.

He was followed by a girl selling flowers. 'All a-growin'! All a-blowin'!' she called out. Again Maisie appeared and after some discussion bought a large bunch of daffodils.

Minutes later the butcher's boy arrived carrying a tray of meat on his head. Since it was uncovered,

Jenkins could see there were chops and kidneys and tripe. His mouth watered at the thought of lunch, but the next moment a low-flying pigeon let free a stream of excrement that landed *splat!* on the meat and Jenkins promptly lost his appetite. But the butcher's boy, unaware of what had happened, tripped down the area steps whistling a cheerful tune.

After an hour of this Jenkins had grown bored. Apart from Maisie, nobody had come out of the Sterlings' house and nobody had gone in. A face had appeared at a first-floor window, a woman – was it Mrs Sterling, he wondered, that shameless creature, looking for her fellow conspirator? – but the curtain had quickly been drawn, suggesting that whoever it was had seen him watching. Surely not, he thought, for he took great pride in his self-confessed amazing ability to conceal himself while keeping a close eye on the activities of suspected criminals.

Another hour went by. There were more people about now, cooks hurrying to market, nannies leading or carrying small children, footmen delivering messages, kitchen maids scrubbing and whitening front steps, well-dressed women stepping into or out of smart carriages . . . Two or three men wan-

dered into the square to smoke a pipe or have a chat, but none looked suspicious.

Though he fought against it, Jenkins could feel his eyelids growing heavier and heavier as the day got hotter. His youngest child, a colicky girl less than a year old, had kept him and his wife awake all night with her agonized screams, and he longed for sleep. He yawned, closed his eyes for a second, yawned again . . . and nodded off.

He was woken minutes later by a sharp tap on the shoulder.

'Here, what the . . .!' In his alarm Jenkins fell backwards, sprawling on the ground.

A constable stood over him, hands on hips. 'What're you up to, lurking in the bushes, eh?' he demanded.

'I'm an officer of the law,' protested Jenkins, scrambling awkwardly to his feet, red-faced with anger and embarrassment.

'Oh yes?' drawled the constable. 'It isn't the first time I've heard that one. Get yourself a smart coat and top hat and try to pass yourself off as a plain-clothes policeman. It's an old dodge, but you can't fool me. I know a villain when I see one. I've been watching you this past hour watching that house . . .' He pointed at the Sterlings' residence.

'Planning to burgle it, are you? Just waiting for the right moment?'

'See this,' exclaimed Jenkins, waving his sergeant's badge in front of the younger man's startled face.

'Oh Lor'. Begging your pardon, sergeant, sir. I didn't realize . . . I mean, I thought . . .'

'What's your name?' barked Jenkins, who was seriously discomfited.

'Parsons, sir. Percival Parsons. And I'm truly sorry, indeed I am. You see, I thought you were . . .'

'All right, all right, Parsons, enough of that.'

'If you don't mind my asking, sir, seeing as how this is my beat –' Parsons indicated the square with his truncheon – 'I'd be much obliged if you'd tell me why you're watching that house so close.'

Jenkins chewed his bottom lip. He would have liked to tell the young upstart to go about his business and leave important affairs to his superior officers, but if it so happened that he had to arrest Mrs Sterling and her accomplice, it would be useful to have a strong young man by his side in case they put up a fight, which they almost certainly would.

'Well, it's like this, Parsons . . .' And in a few words he explained the situation. 'It's my belief that the man we're looking for won't be back till nightfall.

As for the woman, I reckon she'll sit tight, which is what I intend to do. And you'd best be on your way, constable. Do your rounds same as normal. We mustn't let them know we're on to them.'

'Very well, sergeant,' said Parsons. And he walked away, swinging his truncheon.

Jenkins, meanwhile, hunkered down in the bushes again. It was a pity about Parsons, he thought; the young man had made an unnecessary fuss, but no one had observed them. He was quite sure of that. The tramp curled up under the tree looked dead to the world. And for all Jenkins knew, he might well have been, for many people died of sickness and starvation on the streets of London.

The tramp had watched Jenkins ever since he had stolen into the square and concealed his portly form in the bushes. Concealed? The tramp could barely stop himself laughing out loud. Jenkins was an amateur, as inept as a little kid playing hide-and-seek. Anyone with their wits about them could have detected him lurking there. Once he had even fallen asleep . . . And then that young constable had pounced on him. What a joke, one policeman trying to arrest another. And now they were playing spies again, the constable walking round the square, feigning nonchalance, the sergeant peering through the foliage.

Blast them! He hissed in exasperation, turned over and began snoring loudly again, never taking his eyes off Sergeant Jenkins, never for one moment.

56

The Thames was full of boats of every description as far as the eye could see, all going upstream with the tide, barges laden with hay for London's thousands of horses, Whitby cats loaded with coal from the northeast, steam-powered boats with revolving paddles on each side, wherries and scullers conveying the citizens of London across and up and down the river, two-masted brigs and fruit schooners, three-masted barques and clippers from exotic climes carrying tea, coffee, sugar, rice, tobacco and alcohol for London's nourishment and pleasure.

'Which one's the boat we're after?' cried Henry, running to the landing stage at the end of the jetty. 'Oh look, there she is. See!' he pointed excitedly. 'The one with the blue sails. Oh crikey, she's on her way. Come on, you lot, get in or we'll lose her,' he shouted, leaping into the wherry and grabbing an oar.

Gran and Kate stepped aboard more gingerly, for

neither had been in a boat before and they feared it would sink under their weight.

'Don't worry, Kate,' said Henry, as she gripped the sides with white-knuckled fists. 'I've been rowin' this boat for nigh on five years and I'm not dead yet. All right, Jem,' he turned to the boy, 'take the other oar and start rowin' . . . Nah, not like that, you've got to turn the paddles sideways,' he said, resisting the temptation to laugh as Jem fell sprawling on his back. 'Now you're featherin' it,' he said, as Jem's oar skimmed the water, sending up a spray that drenched the others.

'I'm drownin',' wailed Kate 'I thought you said you could row, you varmint.'

'Put the oar in the water, Jem, not on it . . . That's right. You're doin' better now. Keep goin' like that,' said Henry approvingly as the wherry surged forward.

'Where's that boat goin'?' asked Gran, squinting the better to see *La Gaviota* as she sped ahead of them. 'Is it goin' back to Spain?'

'Oh crimes!' gasped Kate. 'We're not goin' there, are we?'

'Course not,' laughed Henry. 'She's full of oranges so she'll be headin' for the Fresh Wharf to unload them before she goes home. We're in luck that her cargo's fruit cos it'll be easier to get to her on the wharves. If she'd been carryin' something like rum or ivory that costs a fortune she'd have put into one of the docks, the West India most like, but we couldn't have got in . . . Nah, it'll be much easier gettin' Billy off her now. But what's he doin' there? That's what I'd like to know.'

'He's been nabbed, that's what,' said Jem. 'I reckon they're goin' to make him work for them . . . and for nothin',' he added bitterly.

'Work? Billy?' scoffed Kate. 'They've got the wrong kid, if you ask me. That little varmint's never done a day's work in his life.'

Slithe, crouching by the jetty, watched them go, a frown creasing the dry, scaly skin on his forehead. One of the girls was rowing and, despite her first few clownish attempts, rowing well. She was strong, very strong for a girl. And suddenly he knew why, for in falling over she had lost her bonnet . . . The girl was a boy, a short, stocky boy with an urchin haircut and black eyes . . . Slithe writhed in fury. It was Jem Perkinski. The boy he was looking for had been right under his nose all the time.

'Blast him!' he swore.

There was a group of watermen waiting for

passengers at the foot of the stairs, strong, weather-beaten men, some chatting, some dozing. But Slithe would not approach them, for watermen were known for their unruly behaviour, their quick wit that frequently turned to rudeness, causing gentle-men to rebuke them, if they dared, and ladies to blush. Slithe knew what would happen if they saw him . . . the jeering, the spiteful taunts, the kicks and blows. But to one side, quite alone, lost in a reverie, sat another waterman, older than the others, a loner by the look of him.

Slithe glided towards him and hissed, 'Old man!'

The waterman turned, saw him, gasped in horror and reached for a crucifix around his neck, muttering a prayer. 'What d'you want?' he said, clambering to his feet and backing away from Slithe.

'I want you to take me to—'

'Nah, not me. I'm not takin' the likes of you nowhere. With a mug like yours . . .? Nah, it'd bring me bad luck.'

'But I have the money . . .'

'I don't care if you've got the Crown jewels. I'm not doin' it and that's my last word.'

'You speak true, my friend,' said Slithe. And he leaped at the waterman, pressing a dagger to his

throat. 'If you refuse me again, it will indeed be your last word on this earth. Well?'

'All right, guv,' gasped the man, his eyes bulging from his head in fright. 'I'll take you. Where d'you want to go?'

'You see that boat, the one with the old woman and girl in it? Follow it. Keep close, but not so close that they suspect we're after them.'

'But that's a wherry, and there're two boys rowin' it. I can't keep up with them, guv, not in a sculler.'

'Then you have a choice,' said Slithe with a smile that turned the waterman's blood to ice. 'You can keep up – or die.'

57

'Could you stop a minute, Henry?' Kate whimpered as the wherry pulled into the middle of the river. 'I want to get out.'

'Don't be a goosecap, Kate,' said Gran. 'You can't get out now. You'll sink to the bottom and drown.'

Kate peered fearfully over the side. 'Is it a long way down?' she said.

'Course it is. And once you're down your body fills with water so's you blow up like a balloon,' said Jem, 'and your eyes pop out of your head and—'

'Stow it!' cried Kate, putting her hands over her ears to block out the horror.

'It isn't true, Kate,' said Henry in an attempt to comfort her. 'You body doesn't swell up. I've seen loads of stiffs and they're all grey and shrivelled like . . .' He looked round for something to compare them with. 'Like your Gran,' he said.

The old lady was so incensed by this she quite forgot she was in a boat, and getting to her feet she

made to give Henry a good whack. But just then a steamer scudded by, sending the wherry pitching and rolling in its choppy wake and Gran, caught off balance, wobbled precariously for a moment and then with a 'Lawks a mercy!' fell overboard.

'You're in luck, guv,' the waterman said to Slithe as they smoothly pulled away from the water's edge, for he may have been old but he was an experienced oarsman. 'That's slowed them down a treat. By the time they get that old trout back on board we'll have caught up with them.'

58

Charles Sterling seldom if ever went anywhere by boat, preferring his own comfortable, reliable carriages to convey him. And, if pressed, he would have confessed that he felt safer on dry land. Water was an alien element, capricious, dangerous, rather like the men whose working habitat it was, he thought, watching with some consternation as a group of them hurried towards him, shouting in rough, raucous voices . . .

'Oars! Sculls! Oars!'

'Where're you goin', guv?'

'I'll take you for less than the rest.'

'Nah, take my boat, guv. It's the best on the river.'

'Best? Paff! It's a leaky old tub. Take mine.'

They pushed and jostled each other, so desperate were they for Mr Sterling's custom. Only fifty years earlier those same men would have charged him two shillings just to cross the river – and told him where to go if he'd balked at the cost – but now they were hungry, for steamboats were taking their trade, and they competed with each other like hyenas around a kill.

'I'm looking for an empty boat,' said Mr Sterling, gripping the handle of his briefcase tightly as they pressed about him.

'Well, you've got plenty to choose from here, guv,' they said, pointing to the dozens of wherries and scullers lying idle.

'No, you misunderstand me. I am looking for an empty boat in the river.' Mr Sterling indicated the middle of the river. 'Out there.'

'Lor',' muttered one of the watermen, 'this one's lost his marbles.'

'Off his chump, I reckon,' said another.

'Cracky.'

And they began to wander away.

'Please!' Mr Sterling pleaded. 'It is imperative that I find the empty boat. I will pay you hand-somely. I will pay you a shilling.'

But they turned their backs on him, for they were superstitious men and feared that carrying a demented man in their boat would bring them ill luck.

'I'll take him,' said a young waterman. 'If someone'll lend me their boat, I'll take the barmy old
codger and split the fare.'

'Where's your boat then, Shep?' one of them
asked.

'Henry's got it. Him and me've had a ruckus.'

'All right. You can take mine. But I want my
share, mind. Don't go playin' none of your tricks
on me.'

'You can trust me,' said Shep, winking. And stepping up to Mr Sterling he said, 'I'll take you, guv. I'll
do it for two shillin's.'

'Two?' said Mr Sterling, taken aback by such an
outrageous demand.

'Not a penny less.'

'Oh, very well.'

'Take that case for you, guv?'

'No. No,' said Mr Sterling, hugging it to his chest.
'No, I can manage, thank you.'

And ignoring Shep's outstretched hand, he
stepped aboard the boat.

59

Detective Inspector Craddock fared better than Mr Sterling and the Perkinskis, for he travelled down-river from Waterloo in one of the fifteen rowing galleys manned by the Thames Division. Under the supervision of a surveyor the oarsmen untethered one of the boats swinging at their moorings below the police stairs and rowed it out into the swirling current.

'The spring tides can be very dangerous,' the surveyor explained to Craddock, 'so I take the boat into the deepest part of the river. We come to less harm there.'

Craddock looked at the three police watermen. In their blue reefer jackets, broad-cut trousers and boaters they looked more like sailors from a Royal Navy man-of-war than constables, and indeed they were all from a marine or seafaring background. Long hours of pulling on the heavy oars in all weathers had hardened them into men of iron and

Craddock felt little harm would come to him in their company. The danger was waiting for him at the Fresh Wharf.

60

Percival Parsons was thrilled. Ever since the Metropolitan Police had formed a Detective Division in 1842 he had set his heart on being a detective. Some people disapproved of detectives because they didn't wear a uniform, calling them spies and snoops, saying it was wrong to fool the public that way, but Parsons didn't agree. He knew they were doing important, vital work in catching some of the craftier criminals. And now, here he was, working with a real, live detective sergeant on an exciting case. Of course, it was a pity he'd pounced on him like that but, after all, Jenkins was in plain clothes so how was he to know the man was a policeman? The important thing was to put that unfortunate incident behind him and impress Jenkins with his efficiency so that he would recommend him for promotion.

Jenkins watched the young constable with increasing alarm. What was the foolish pup up to, peering

 293

over the railings into every area, staring in at windows, stopping everyone he met and asking what they were doing in the square, even those who clearly lived and worked there? And now, Jenkins groaned inwardly, Parsons was sniffing around every bush and shrub in the vicinity. He'll be cross-examining the trees next, Jenkins thought angrily. Short of proclaiming in a loud voice, 'I'm a policeman looking for a possible criminal,' Parsons could not have been more obvious if he'd tried.

Jenkins was just making a mental note to put in a report to the supervisor of C Division, to whom Parsons reported, to the effect that the young constable was one of the most clumsy and inept officers he had ever had the misfortune to work with when Parsons stumbled on the tramp, still hidden in the undergrowth, snoring.

'Move along there, my good man,' he said.

The tramp was an unsavoury character. His coat looked and smelled as if he had slept in it for years and in his long beard could clearly be seen the remains of many a meal — bits of bread, cheese, potato, sausage, watercress, even a winkle or two. In addition to his other shortcomings he also appeared to be deaf, for he continued to sleep despite Parsons'

insistent threat that if he didn't move he would be arrested.

Parsons reached down and tapped him on the shoulder. 'If you don't get on your way this instant,' he boomed, 'you will be taken into custody.' And he gave the man a jab in the ribs with his foot to reinforce his threat.

Jenkins was incensed by this piece of gross misconduct on the part of a police officer. Parsons was bellowing, 'Move along!' for the umpteenth time at the inert tramp, and Jenkins was emerging from his hiding place to take control of the situation, swearing under his breath because Parsons had forced him to break cover, when the door of the Sterlings' house opened and Mrs Sterling came running towards them, crying, 'Stop! Stop! Leave him alone!'

As soon as he heard her voice the tramp leaped up, snarled, 'You fool, Flo!' and took off across the square with an amazing turn of speed.

The young constable followed, springing his rattle and yelling, 'Stop that man! Stop him!' But Jenkins stayed where he was, his feelings of anger turning to smug satisfaction. Putting a firm hand on Mrs Sterling's shoulder to prevent her from running as well, he said, 'Now then, madam, what's all this about, eh?'

61

By the time Henry and Jem had fished Gran out of the water with a boathook and grapnel *La Gaviota* was almost out of sight.

'Drat!' Henry fumed. 'We're goin' to lose her.'

But luck was on their side, for the wind suddenly dropped and all the sailing ships on the river were becalmed, their jibs and spinnakers hanging idly from the masts.

'Jammy!' he exclaimed, well pleased. But Gran was not. No man or woman, respectable or otherwise, would ever appear in public without some form of headgear, no matter how dilapidated, and boots, even if they were down at heel with the soles hanging off.

'I've lost my bonnet,' the old lady fretted. 'And —' she looked at her bare feet, the corns and bunions turning blue with cold — 'my lovely satin shoes fell off.'

'Lor's sake, Kate, give her your bonnet,' said Jem.

'Only if you give her your boots,' retorted Kate.

'Here, Gran, put this on to keep you warm,' said Henry, taking off his jacket and handing it to the old lady. But she was still not content.

'I'm feelin' a bit peaky. I could do with somethin' strong to pick me up,' she said, looking hopefully at Henry.

'I don't keep booze in the boat,' he said.

'What? Not even a drop of gin to keep the cold out?'

Henry laughed. 'Rowin' hard keeps the cold out.'

'I've got somethin' for you, Gran,' said Kate. 'You'll be right as ninepence after a swig of this.' And she drew from her pocket a bottle of the Miracle of Life.

'Paff!' exclaimed the old lady, waving it away in disgust. 'I wouldn't touch that muck if I was dyin'!'

Jem was beginning to get the hang of rowing by now and as he and Henry pulled doggedly on the oars the wherry skimmed across the water, dodging in and out of the bigger, heavier craft until they were almost level with *La Gaviota*. But when the skittish wind started blowing again she and all the other two- and three-masters surged forward, leaving the rowing boat far behind.

Despite this setback there was great excitement on board, for above the slap of waves against the side of the wherry a distinct sound could be heard.

'Did you hear him?' shouted Henry. 'A little kid bawlin' for his ma!'

'It's Billy,' cried Jem. 'I'd know that squally voice anywhere. It's Billy!'

62

'You lookin' for a particular empty boat, guv, or will any one do?' said Shep as he rowed Mr Sterling towards the middle of the river.

'I believe it to be a rowing boat,' said Mr Sterling.

'And what're you goin' to do when you find it, may I ask?'

'I shall place this in it.' Mr Sterling tapped the case on his lap.

'And are you goin' to get in as well?' said Shep, doing his best to conduct a normal conversation with Mr Sterling even though it was quite obvious the man was raving mad.

'No, I shall return to the stairs with you.'

Shep eyed the case greedily. Even empty, he thought, it was a nice piece of leather that would fetch at least a shilling in the market. But no one would carry an empty case, would they? There had to be something in it, something of value, surely?

There and then he formed a plan to get the old

lunatic back to the quay as fast as he could and return for the case. But first he had to find the empty boat.

'I see it, guv. I do see it,' he said, pointing at a sculler cockling and spinning towards them on the tide. And, shipping his oars, he waited for it to come alongside.

63

'Ah, I see my man,' said Craddock, watching Mr Sterling through a pair of binoculars. 'He's approaching the empty boat . . . He's putting the case on board. Slow down, please,' he said to the surveyor. 'The kidnappers must not know we are watching or Clara will be in great danger.'

'Easy all. Easy,' said the surveyor, bringing the galley to a halt. 'What do you want me to do now, inspector?'

'I should like you to – What the devil?' exclaimed Craddock.

'What have you seen?'

'Another empty rowing boat.'

'And another one, sir,' said one of the police watermen, pointing.

'And another.'

To Craddock's amazement at least half a dozen empty rowing boats were bobbing along in the wake of the first at regular intervals.

'Looks as if the kidnappers are playing some kind of game,' said the surveyor. 'Could it be that they know we're on to them and are trying to confuse us?'

'I think you're right,' agreed Craddock. 'Surveyor, be so good as to instruct your men to pull alongside one of those boats.'

'For what purpose, may I ask?'

'So that I may get in it.'

'To search it?'

'No, surveyor, to row it.'

The other man frowned. 'You're surely not intending to row it yourself, sir?'

'I am.'

'Have you ever rowed on the river before?'

'Never.'

'The current can be very dangerous, not to mention the huge amount of traffic. The river's no place for an amateur, especially in weather like this,' said the surveyor, for the day that had started so bright had suddenly turned sullen. Black clouds appeared overhead, and with flashes of lightning and claps of thunder they emptied their load of water in a torrential downpour. In an instant all was chaos on the river, with crews hurrying to cover their cargoes with tarpaulins. 'You'll have trouble handling a boat in these conditions,' said the surveyor sternly, as the icy rain drove into their faces like stair rods, almost blinding them.

'I am well aware of that,' said Craddock, who had seen many a body dragged from the river's depths, 'but since I'm in plain clothes and you and your men are in a very conspicuous uniform, I fancy I shall do better on my own from now on.'

'Just as you wish, sir,' said the surveyor with a resigned air. 'But should you need us we shall be standing by at a discreet distance. You have only to give us the nod.'

'Thank you,' said Craddock. And stepping gingerly into one of the empty row boats, he seized the oars and rowed away with a great deal of muttering and splashing.

64

Florence Sterling burst into floods of tears as Constable Parsons chased after the tramp, and it was some time before she could speak.

'That man . . .' she sobbed. 'That man . . .'

'Kidnapped your daughter, Clara, did he not?' said Sergeant Jenkins, his face expressing his disgust.

The woman's eyes opened wide and she stared at him aghast.

'Come along, Mrs Sterling, it's time to tell the truth – the whole truth, mind,' said Jenkins, still keeping a tight hold of her.

'That man . . .' she blurted out. 'That man is Clara's father.'

'Her . . .?'

'Father.'

'You mean he's your . . .?'

'Husband.'

'But you're married to . . .?'

'Mr Sterling.'

'So you have . . . ?'

'Two husbands.'

'Madam –' Sergeant Jenkins drew himself up, puffed out his chest and addressed her with the full force of the law – 'I am arresting you for the crime of bigamy.'

And snapping handcuffs on her, he led the weeping woman away.

305

65

'Jammy! The tide's high so she can tie up right alongside the quay,' said Henry, watching *La Gaviota* as she edged her way through the tangle of shipping at the Fresh Wharf. 'That'll make it dead easy for us. All we have to do is get aboard when no one's around.'

'*No one's around?* You must be kiddin', 'Enry,' said Kate, for despite the torrential downpour the wharf was seething with men, unshaven, weather-beaten men in thick jackets and thigh boots, shouting and whistling signals to each other as seagulls screamed overhead. Kate had never seen so much frenzied activity, not even in Devil's Acre on a Saturday night when the pubs turned out – lightermen rowing back and forth between the big ships moored in the river, unloading their cargo; wharfingers and porters loading it into carts for onward transmission to warehouses, markets and shops; sailors gabbling in a dozen different languages, excited to be on land again, if only for a short time.

'And what about them?' said Jem, pointing to the police patrolling the wharf, swinging their truncheons.

'There aren't that many, not like at the docks. There they've got so much stuff worth nickin' the place is stiff with crushers and guards. Run you in soon as look at you, they would. But here?' he shrugged. 'Who'd want to nick oranges – apart from Shep?' he added drily. 'But then he'd nick the nose off your face if he thought he could get anythin' for it.'

'So what do we do now?' said Kate nervously.

'Wait till it's real dark,' said Jem.

'Yeh,' Henry agreed. 'In this weather all the workers'll go home in a while and the sailors'll go off to the taverns. That's when we'll make our move.'

'What d'you want me to do now, guv?' said the old waterman, slumped over his oars, his breath coming in wheezing gulps as he stopped short of Henry's wherry.

'You can do whatever you like, old man,' sniggered Slithe. And before the waterman could say,

'Oy, what about my money then?' his passenger had slipped over the side and swum away into the cold, dark murk like some monstrous sea serpent.

66

Mr Sterling had gone back to Victoria Square, his emotions ricocheting between hope and despair. As the horse wended its way through the wet streets he reached up time and again and tapped on the roof of the hansom cab to tell the driver to stop, for he had seen yet another group of sodden urchins begging for their supper and a night's shelter from the evil weather. Eager hands reached out to him and in every one he put a coin, as if by helping them he was in some way helping Clara. The memory of her face the first time he had seen her in the rookery came back to him now as he looked into the gaunt, hollow-eyed faces of the children surrounding the cab and his eyes filled with tears. And when he got home there was yet more sadness awaiting him.

'Oh, sir,' cried Mrs Restall, hurrying to greet him when Maisie opened the front door, 'I don't know how to tell you this . . .'

'Is it Clara? Have they found her? Have they . . . ?'

'No, there's no news of the girl, sir. But Mrs Sterling . . . She's been arrested. They've taken her to Scotland Yard.'

67

The visibility on the river was so poor Craddock could barely see ten yards ahead of him. He wiped his eyes with a dripping handkerchief and swore vehemently about the vagaries of the English climate. 'One minute it's sunny and the next . . .' He scowled at the black clouds and never-ending downpour . . . 'this!'

To make matters worse, the tide had begun to turn, sweeping everything downriver towards the Thames Estuary. Logs rolled and drifted in the swirling current. Flotsam and jetsam slapped against the banks. Once Craddock nearly lost an oar and the boat spun round like a top. But he never took his eyes off Shep, who was rowing eagerly up to every empty boat and looking inside.

'Not found it yet, eh?' snarled Craddock. 'Not found the one you're looking for, with the ransom money in it? But you will sooner or later. And when you do I'll be right behind you.' He smiled grimly. 'And I'll make sure it's transportation for you, my boy – or worse.'

68

In the deepening twilight Jem and Henry rowed the wherry as close as they dared to the Fresh Wharf and tied her up.

'You'd best wait here,' Jem told Gran and Kate, 'till we come back.'

'What did you think we were goin' to do? Go for a swim?' replied the old lady.

'What if the crushers see us?' said Kate nervously.

'Tell them you're fishin'.'

'What, in the dark?'

'There's no law against fishin' in the dark.'

'But it's rainin'.'

'There's no law against fishing in the rain neither.'

'But we haven't got nothin' to fish with.'

'There are rods under the seat,' said Henry. 'Me and Shep often do a bit of fishin' for our supper when we can't get no customers.'

'But I don't know how.'

'It's easy, Kate. All you do is—'

'Oh dry up, Lor's sake!' grumbled Jem. 'We're supposed to be rescuin' Billy, not teachin' Kate how to catch varminty fish.'

'Listen!' said Gran, clutching his arm. 'Listen!'

From one of the boats came the sound of a child crying for its mother.

'It's Billy! Go! Go plaguy quick and get him!'

Jem and Henry climbed out of the wherry and crept along the quayside, dodging behind wooden barrels and stacks of crates whenever a policeman or one of the guards employed by the Fresh Wharf hove into view.

'Which one's the Spanish boat?' whispered Jem, for although there were oil lamps at intervals along the quayside and on the boats, it was difficult to make out one from the other in the deep, dark shadows.

'There she is,' Henry pointed. 'And we're in luck, Jem. Look, they're all leavin'.'

Unaware that they were being watched, Matilde and Paco disembarked with the rest of their crew to roam the sleazy streets and dingy alleyways behind the wharves, looking for pubs and food stalls and seeking refuge from the downpour. And since their

314

cargo had little appeal to thieves, they left it in the care of just one sailor – and his cutlass.

'*Watch those kids,*' Matilde said to him, pointing at the tarpaulin, tied at both ends now to prevent Clara and Billy from escaping. '*Keep a close eye on them. Especially the girl. She's a little devil.*'

'*We'll soon be rid of her,*' said Paco.

Matilde nodded. '*The Master said we must wait until we're ready to sail, then drug the girl and hide her in one of the crates where her doting father will find her – but not until we are well clear.*'

'*And the boy?*'

'*The Master said he is ours to do with what we want, as long as we never bring him back to this country. He will be useful on the voyage. He can wash dishes, scrub decks, clean the brass, polish the wood. And when we get him home to Jerez he will be our servant.*' Matilde cackled. '*Nobody will understand him complaining in English. He can moan all he likes.*'

Paco shook his head doubtfully. '*I'm afraid he'll give us trouble,*' he said.

'*If he does –*' Matilde shrugged – '*we'll feed him to the fishes.*'

Slithe followed the two boys at a discreet distance, slinking from shadow to shadow, more monster than man, his eyes glittering at the thought of the foul deed he was about to commit.

Drawing his dagger from his sleeve, he brought the steely tip to his lips in a gruesome kiss and whispered, 'Now, my friend, the moment has come at last. Now you will slide deep into Jem Perkinski's heart and silence him forever.'

Shep had found the case. Craddock watched as he reached over and lifted it into his own wherry, pushing the other boat away.

'Now, my friend,' Craddock growled, 'the moment has come at last.' And heaving on the oars, he made for Shep's skiff, ramming it so hard he almost capsized it.

'What the . . . ?' the waterman cried out in alarm.

'Police!' Craddock shouted, producing his tipstaff. 'Come aboard and bring the case with you. Now!'

'I've not done nothin' wrong, guv,' whined Shep. 'A gen'leman said he'd left his case in a boat and asked me to go and get it for him, so I—'

'Enough of your lies!' Craddock barked. 'We both know what's in that case.'

'I don't, guv. I swear on my mother's life I don't know. The gent didn't tell me.'

316

'Open it! Well, don't just sit there gawping at me. I said, open it.'

Still stunned by his misfortune and protesting his innocence, Shep opened the case a fraction to protect its contents from the rain and peered inside.

'Blimey!' he breathed.

'You're a poor actor,' sneered Craddock, although the look of sheer amazement on Shep's face belied his words. 'Well?'

'It's full of money, guv.'

'Is it now?' said Craddock sarcastically. 'And how much is in there? Two thousand, would you say?'

'Two thous . . . ?' For a fleeting moment it crossed Shep's mind that for such a huge sum it would be worth trying to overcome Craddock, knock him senseless, throw him in the drink and make off for France or some other foreign parts where nobody would ever find him . . . But Craddock looked like a formidable opponent, and as if he knew what Shep was thinking he took an evil-looking bludgeon from his pocket and nodded over his shoulder, indicating the river police waiting at the ready with their cutlasses and pistols.

Uttering a deep sigh at the cruel twist of fate that had put an unimaginable fortune into his hands only to snatch it away, Shep reached into the case and riffled his wet fingers through the notes for the sheer pleasure of caressing so much money. And then his expression changed. Turning the case so that Craddock could see inside, he lifted up the four five-pound notes on top to reveal sheets and sheets of blank paper underneath. 'There's only twenty quid in here,' he said.

'What a disappointment for you,' replied Craddock, his voice heavy with sarcasm.

'Disappointment?'

'Did you really think that a man as shrewd as Mr Sterling would give in to your demands? It is he who has played a clever trick on you, my friend.'

'Mr Sterling?' Shep looked mystified. 'I don't know who you're talkin' about.'

'Paff!' Craddock exclaimed contemptuously. 'Don't act the fool with me. Tell me who is behind this villainy and I promise you you'll get a lighter sentence.'

'What villainy?

Losing patience with Shep, Craddock tapped him on the shoulder with his tipstaff and said, 'I am arresting you for the kidnapping of Clara Sterling.'

Shep's face fell. 'Kidnappin'?' he cried. 'I've never kidnapped nobody in my life, guv. Honest!'

69

As abruptly as it had started, the rain stopped and the sky cleared to reveal a full moon that bathed the world in its soft light.

'Drat!' groaned Henry. 'That's just what we didn't want. Now that sailor on *La Gaviota* 'll see us.'

'But it's two to one, us against him,' said Jem.

'Yeh, but he's got a cutlass.'

'And we've got brains and fists. We'll get on the boat and . . .'

'Oh yeh? And how're we goin' to do that?' said Henry, for to make sure that no one could board *La Gaviota* while her captain and crew were away, the sailor left on guard had pulled up the gangplank.

'We've got to find another way,' said Jem. 'What about them?' He pointed at the mooring lines holding *La Gaviota* to the bollards on the quay. 'We could climb up them and . . .'

'What, them ropes?' scoffed Henry. 'What d'you take me for? A monkey?'

'I can do it,' said Jem, who'd never climbed a rope in his life, especially one hanging over cold, dark water. 'It's dead easy.'

'Yeh, well, so can I. I was just kiddin',' said Henry, who didn't want to lose face in front of the much younger, smaller boy.

'Jammy!' Jem beamed. 'I'll go up the front end and you go up the back.'

'The bow and the stern,' Henry corrected him.

'Yeh, right. And when we're on, I'll shout or do somethin' to attract that sailor's attention and you jump on him from behind and I'll grab his cutlass and you—'

'All right, I've got it.' Henry nodded eagerly. 'I don't think we'll have much trouble with him.' He indicated the Spanish sailor, who was gabbling incoherently and singing snatches of song in a maudlin voice. 'Sounds as if he's lushy already.'

The man was indeed drunk. He leaned against the main mast, a bottle of rum in his hand, gazing wistfully at the bright lights in the distance, the oil lamps and candles flickering in tavern windows along the shoreline, and bemoaning his luck at having drawn the short straw to guard *La Gaviota*. So engrossed was he in his drunken rendition of a Spanish love song that he neither heard nor saw the two boys as they slipped and slithered up the wet ropes and stole on to the deck until Jem shouted at him, 'Oy, you, knocker-face! Over here!'

Bellowing with rage, the sailor lurched unsteadily towards him, drawing his cutlass . . . and stopped, staring wide-eyed with horror at something above Jem's head.

'*Madre de Dios!*' he cried, crossing himself. '*It's Satan. It's the serpent. May God protect me.*' And screaming in terror, he jumped overboard.

Jem looked up to see what had frightened the sailor and his heart stopped. There, wrapped around the mast like a venomous tree snake, his eyes afire, his tongue flickering over dry, cracked lips, was Slithe.

'Now, Jem Perkinski, I have you,' he gloated. And drawing his dagger he slid down the mast, down and down and round and round, reaching the deck in a trice, hissing, 'Kill! Kill! Kill!'

Henry was so petrified by this fearful apparition he couldn't move, but Jem was made of sterner stuff. He looked round for a way of escape . . . Back down the mooring line? Up one of the masts? No. Slithe would catch him. For one desperate moment he considered jumping overboard too, but he couldn't swim. There was only one place to go – the crew's quarters.

Down the companionway he went, half stumbling over his skirt, half falling. In the pale light filtering through the grimy portholes he made out two lines of bunks three tiers high down each side of the cramped cabin. Quickly he scrambled into a top one and flattened himself against the straw mattress, holding his breath as an eerie figure glided down the stairs and slid its scaly hands over each bunk. Jem knew the disgusting reptile would find him in a second and the dagger he could see now, glinting evilly in the moonlight, would penetrate his heart. But . . . But there was something sticking in his stomach, something hard. Stealthily he slid his hand down until his fingers closed over it. A flagon! The sailors had been drinking heavily before they set off for their night's entertainment and left empty wine flagons on their bunks. Jem gripped its neck and as Slithe turned towards him brought it down hard on his head.

Slithe slumped to the floor, writhing in pain, but the blow had only stunned him and after a moment to recover from the shock he leaped after Jem as the boy sprang up the narrow stairway. Henry, who had finally recovered his senses, ran across the deck, and as Jem shot out of the companionway like a ball from a cannon he slammed the door shut and bolted it.

'Master! Master, help me!' Slithe shrieked. 'Help me!'

'Crimes, what is it?' said Henry, recoiling in horror as Slithe howled and hammered on the door.

'It's . . . It's the slimy creature that nabbed Clara and Billy,' gasped Jem. 'But where are they?'

As if on cue a little voice cried, 'Ma, I want my ma!'

70

It took four of the wharf policemen to restrain Slithe so that Craddock could question him.

'Who are you?' he demanded.

'Slithe.'

'Is that your first or last name?'

'Just Slithe.'

'And where are you from?'

'Hell.'

Craddock grimaced. It was as much as he could do to look at the vile creature writhing on the deck of *La Gaviota*.

'You have committed a serious offence. You tried to harm that young boy.'

'Jem Perkinski.' Slithe spat out the name. 'I should have killed him. The Master told me to.'

'The Master?' Craddock frowned. 'Who is the Master?'

Slithe sneered by way of answer and looked away.

'This . . . er . . . man, inspector,' said one of the policemen holding Slithe down. 'I recognize him from the description witnesses have given. It's my belief he's . . .'

'The Snake. Yes, I agree, constable.' Craddock nodded. 'I have no doubt we have captured the Snake at last.'

'But who's this Master he keeps on about, sir?'

'I will never betray him,' hissed Slithe. 'You will never know his name.'

'Ah, but I already do,' said Craddock grimly. And bending forward, he whispered in Slithe's ear.

'No! No!' Slithe shrieked, his face torn between fear and grief. 'Oh my brother, my brother, my poor brother.'

71

'Married?' echoed Mr Sterling, scarcely believing his ears. 'Is it true, Florence? Are you married to another man?'

'The lady admitted as much to me, sir,' said Sergeant Jenkins, looking at her with stern disapproval.

Mrs Sterling hung her head in shame. 'I thought Joe, my husband, was dead,' she said in a voice so faint the two men had to lean towards her to hear it. 'He was put in clink just before Pip was born and they told me he'd been killed in a brawl, and I believed it cos he was always a violent man. He used to beat me . . .' She closed her eyes as if to block out painful memories. 'But I was walkin' home one day, just a month ago, when he suddenly grabbed me, said he'd been wounded in the fight and left for dead but he'd recovered, said he'd heard how, thinkin' myself a widow, I'd married again. And ever since he's been . . . he's been . . .' She faltered.

'Blackmailing you?' said Mr Sterling angrily.

His wife nodded. 'He said if anyone was to find out about him and me I'd go to prison for bigamy, but if I gave him money he wouldn't tell.'

'The blackguard!' exclaimed Mr Sterling as Sergeant Jenkins nodded in silent agreement.

'I'm sorry. I'm so sorry,' said Mrs Sterling.

'My dearest, it is not your fault. No one could accuse you of deliberately committing a crime. Am I not right, sergeant?'

'Well, sir, it's not for me to give a judgement, but if you want my opinion I'd say any magistrate would feel sympathy for a lady in her predicament. She was misled. No one can blame her for that. In fact, I'd go so far as to say . . . Hello!' He stopped short as the door opened and Craddock came in followed by Jem, Henry, Billy and . . .

'Clara!' cried Mrs Sterling, running to the little girl and sweeping her into her arms. 'Oh Clara, darlin'! My little darlin'!' she wept, hugging her so hard Clara gasped, 'Ma, I can't breathe.'

'Well done, sir,' said Mr Sterling, shaking Craddock warmly by the hand. 'I cannot tell you how grateful I am to you for finding my daughter.'

'Not me, sir. I wasn't the one who found her. It's

these two you must thank for that,' said Craddock, turning to Jem and Henry.

'It was nothin',' muttered Henry.

'Dead easy,' said Jem. 'All I did was crack him on the nut with a bottle . . .'

'And I locked him in so he couldn't get out.'

'Him?' Mr Sterling looked from one to the other. 'Who are we talking about?'

'A vicious criminal, someone the Metropolitan Police has been looking for for some time,' said Craddock. 'He is known as the Snake. You will surely have read about him in the newspapers.'

'Indeed I have, inspector,' said Mr Sterling. 'I understand he is responsible for a number of thefts and brutal murders. But what has he to do with the kidnapping of my daughter?'

'Extracting information from Slithe — the man known as the Snake — has not been easy, since he is of unsound mind, but it seems that everything he has done has been on the instructions of a man to whom he is devoted, a man who helped him escape from Bedlam and launched him on a series of heinous crimes, the last of which were the abductions of your daughter, Clara, and the boys, Billy Perkinski. A man, in fact, whom he has finally admitted is his own brother.'

'Ah!' Mr Sterling sat down heavily. 'I rather think I know the name of that scandalous brother, inspector.'

'Indeed you do, sir.' Craddock nodded gravely. 'You were correct in your assumption. It was a clever ruse, which must have come into his mind when you married. I'm afraid that like Joe –' he glanced at Mrs Sterling, who shook her head angrily at the mention of her first husband – 'he wanted to take advantage of your newfound happiness. He knew how devoted you had become to Clara. All he had to do was lure her to a place where his brother, the Snake, could abduct her and then hide her on *La Gaviota* until the ransom was paid . . .'

'Which meant he would get his money back *and* my company,' said Mr Sterling.

'Who are we talkin' about?' said Mrs Sterling, looking from her husband to the inspector in puzzlement. 'Who is this man?'

'My partner . . . That is to say, my former partner, Septimus Mallick,' said Mr Sterling.

'No, no, you must be wrong, my dear. Not Septimus.'

'I very much regret that he has been the mastermind behind these dastardly crimes,' said Mr Sterling. 'I had suspected him for some time of harbouring a desire to take over my company – behind that affable exterior lurks a very greedy man – and when he offered to buy it in return for paying Clara's ransom my suspicion was sharpened. That is why, with the inspector's agreement –' he glanced at Craddock, who nodded – 'I removed the bank notes from the case he gave me, replacing them with blank sheets with just four five-pound notes on top.'

'So you tricked that greedy man out of a lot of money, Father,' cried Clara, clapping her hands in delight.

'I shall, of course, give the money to charity, since I do not think Septimus will have need of it where he is going,' Mr Sterling chuckled. 'But turning the tables on that villain and retaining my company is nothing to the joy I feel at having you back,' he said, holding out his arms to Clara.

'Where is Septimus now?' demanded Mrs Sterling. 'When I get my hands on him I'll . . .'

'We have him in custody,' said Craddock. 'He was waiting in a boat downriver to pick up the case with the ransom money in it. When arrested he protested that he was "only learning to row",' Craddock said, amid hearty laughter.

'And the Snake?' piped up Billy, shivering at the memory of Slithe's hideous features.

'Under lock and key alongside his brother. And I fancy the two of them will soon be swinging side by side at the end of a rope.'

'And what about me?' said Jem.

'In the circumstances we have decided not to hang you,' said Craddock, straightfaced.

'*What?*' cried Jem. And then he saw the twinkle in the inspector's eye. 'Look here, I rescued Clara – I reckon I should get the reward,' he said.

'Indeed you should, young man,' agreed Mr Sterling, drawing a hundred pounds from his wallet.

'Between the two boys,' said Craddock quickly as Jem grabbed the bank notes.

Grudgingly Jem offered Henry a five-pound note.

'Half, Jem,' said Craddock.

'*What?*'

'Give Henry half. He played an equal part in capturing the Snake and rescuing Clara.'

'But . . .'

'*Half.*'

'Oh, all right,' said Jem, handing over the notes.

'How much is half?' said Billy.

'Fifty pounds,' said Craddock.

'Blimey!' Billy's eyes popped. 'How many pork pies could we buy with that?'

331

'How much do pork pies cost?' asked Craddock, for his wife did all the shopping.

'We can get real crusty, juicy ones for twopence a piece.'

'So, with fifty pounds you could buy six thousand,' said Craddock, grinning.

'Six thousand pork pies?' sighed Billy rapturously. 'That's one a day for the rest of my life.'

'Nah, it isn't,' said Jem.

'Why not?'

'Cos you won't live that long,' said Jem, grabbing him by the scruff of the neck and dragging him away. 'When I tell Ma you sold her tray and all the stuff on it for just one penny, she'll kill you!'

72

With his share of the reward Henry treated Kate to dinner at a smart chop house. To look their very best for the occasion, for they had never eaten anywhere but in their room or on the street, they went to the local market to buy some clothes.

Having spent an hour or more rummaging through the piles of smelly, grubby hand-me-downs, Kate finally chose a riding habit, because someone had told her that riding habits were very fashionable – or had been twenty years earlier – a long dress and jacket with a great deal of tatty gold braid on the collar and epaulettes and a tall hat like a red pillar box with two huge ostrich feathers sagging from the top.

Henry opted for blue and green check trousers, a shirt with ruffs and frills at the neck and wrists, a satin embroidered waistcoat, plum-coloured jacket, full-length black evening cloak and top hat – all of which had seen better days, if not years. But Kate was impressed.

'Lor', 'Enry, you look like Prince Albert himself,' she said, running her fingers over the faded velvet facings on Henry's jacket.

'And you look like the queen, Kate,' said her boyfriend admiringly.

Kate fussed and fretted about whether to carry a muff or a parasol and fan, eventually deciding on all three, and Henry carried a walking stick which had, unfortunately, lost the lion's head that had once adorned it but, 'Nobody'll notice it,' he said, 'cos I'll keep my hand over the broken bit.'

And so they set off, arm in arm, for the chop house, as pleased as punch with their appearance.

The waiter who greeted them was not so appreciative, however. His face fell when they swept in, and if Henry hadn't flashed a handful of notes to show he was able to pay for their meal the waiter might well have put them at a table behind the kitchen door. As it was, in the hope of receiving a handsome tip, he led them, with much bobbing and bowing, to a table in the very centre of the room.

The other diners stared at them, whispering and tittering behind their hands, and one impudent wag shouted, 'Tally ho!' but Kate took their attention to

be flattering. 'They've never seen nobody so well dressed before,' she whispered to Henry. 'I shouldn't be surprised as how we'll get our picture in the newspapers. Front page.'

The waiter offered a menu and stood with increasing impatience as Henry squinted at it, his cheeks turning redder and redder with embarrassment, for although he could draw and paint beautifully and knew everything about boats, he could not read or write.

'I don't know,' he shrugged. 'Er . . .'

'May I suggest,' said the waiter and promptly reeled off a list of dishes that might tempt their palates . . . 'Mock turtle soup, crimped salmon, lobster cutlets, oyster patties, roast pigeon, larded quails, curried rabbit, fillets of hare, Charlotte Russe, compote of cherries, Madeira wine jelly . . .'

'Yeh.' Henry nodded enthusiastically.

'Yes? Yes what, sir?' asked the waiter, puzzled.

'Yeh, we'll have the lot. And a nice plate of cockles and winkles too, my man.'

'And eels,' said Kate. 'Hot eels with plenty of juice.'

'And crumpets,' added Henry. 'Hot crumpets oozin' with butter.'

The waiter blanched. 'And to drink, sir?' he enquired in a faint voice.

'A mug of ginger beer,' said Henry. 'Nah, on second thoughts make that two. I'm that thirsty I could drink the Thames dry.'

'And a lemonade for me, a big'un,' said Kate.

'Certainly, madam,' said the waiter, hurrying away.

Henry and Kate were very hungry, for they were always very hungry, and they made short work of the gargantuan feast, pausing only to let out the occasional hearty belch.

'Golopshus,' said Kate, licking her fingers and drying them on her dress when she'd finished. 'That was a rattlin' good spread.'

'Scrumptious,' agreed Henry. But his face fell when the waiter presented the bill.

'Ten quid?' he exclaimed. 'Blimey, that's more than we spend on grub in a year.'

'You ordered everything on the menu, sir,' said the waiter stiffly.

'And it was worth it,' beamed Kate. 'Lor', if I was a lady and had loads of money, I'd eat like this every night.'

'And so you will, my tulip,' said Henry, 'cos I'm

goin' to be filthy rich one day. My dad's given me the wherry, it's all mine now, and me and Shep—'

'Shep?' Kate said sharply. 'You're not goin' to work with that varminty toerag no more, are you?'

'He's changed, Kate – he has!' insisted Henry as Kate shook her head in disbelief. 'That Inspector Craddock told him he'd put him in clink if he caught him cheatin' and stealin' again and he's given back all the money he stole from Gran.'

'Huh! Only cos he had to.'

'Nah, he's promised to behave proper from now on, Kate. And I'll see to it that he does. I'm the boss – I'm not standin' no more nonsense from him.'

'Oh, 'Enry, you're so strong,' Kate gushed. 'I was real proud of you the way you nabbed the Snake. If I was the queen I'd give you a medal for bein' the bravest man in England.'

'I didn't do it all on my own, Kate,' said Henry, blushing. 'Jem—'

'Jem? Paff! It was you what did it. Oh, 'Enry,' said Kate, gazing at him adoringly, 'you're my 'ero.'

73

Ma was happy. She'd got Billy back safe and sound and Pa was out of hospital. And when she saw the fifty pounds Mr Sterling had given Jem as a reward she was so happy she quite forgave Billy for having sold her tray for a penny.

'Tell you what,' she said. 'Let's have a party to celebrate.'

And they did. That very day. And so many of their relatives and friends and neighbours came that by midnight there was no more room in the yard. In fact, they had to move the pigs out of their sty so that people 'could sit somewhere in comfort', as Ma said.

Jem was resplendent in the jacket, shirt and trousers, with both legs, he'd bought with his share of the prize money. And there were gasps of admiration when he put on his new wideawake, a stunning creation in black felt with a ribbon round the brim.

'I liked you better as a girl,' laughed Ned, neatly avoiding the punch Jem aimed at his nose.

'Tell us again how you caught the Snake, Jem,' said Cousin Annie.

At that everyone stopped chattering to listen, for they were fascinated by the story – especially as it grew more amazing every time Jem told it.

'And then the Snake got me down and near strangled me, but I fought him off and . . . and I climbed up the mast and . . . and I jumped on him. Flattened him, I did.'

'Last time you said the Snake was up the mast and you were on the deck,' said Ned. But nobody heard him because they were all busy congratulating Jem on his extraordinary bravery.

'And you did it all on your own,' said Uncle Arthur, patting him on the back.

'Yeh.' Jem stuck his chest out proudly.

'Nah, you didn't,' protested Ned. ''Enry said that he—'

''Enry? Paff! All he did was help me row the wherry.'

'I reckon you should've got all the reward money, my tulip,' said Ma.

'Yeh, they wanted to give it to me, Ma, seein' as how I caught the Snake singled-handed – well,

339

almost,' he added, casting a warning glance at Ned not to contradict him again or there would be trouble, 'but I said it was only fair that 'Enry should get his share.'

'Well, at least it's still in the family, cos 'Enry's one of us now. And a lucky fellow he is too,' said Pa, beaming gummily at everyone, 'cos I reckon bein' a Perkinski's the jammiest thing that can happen to you.'

'You're right, Bert,' said Uncle Arthur, raising his glass. 'Here's to the Perkinskis.'

'Yeh!' agreed Billy enthusiastically. But nobody heard him because his mouth was full of pork pie.

A Note from the Author

Thames Watermen

For as long as the Thames has been an important economic highway, people have wanted to get from one bank to the other and sturdy, weather-beaten men have been willing, in exchange for a coin or three, to row them across.

By the 1500s there were around four thousand watermen working on the Thames (watermen carried passengers in their boats, lightermen carried goods) and when in 1555 the Company of Watermen and Lightermen was formed, it was one of the largest companies in London.

Life was never easy for a waterman. Apart from the dangers of navigating such a busy, fast-flowing river, the weather was frequently against them. Since the Thames was much wider in centuries past, with many mudflats, it frequently froze over, which put the watermen out of work until the thaw. And summer was little better. The Thames received all London's waste, so that by the mid-nineteenth century it had become an open sewer, the source of the infamous 'Great Stink' of 1858. Nor did the watermen fare well when the press gangs came round to recruit 'volunteers' for the Royal Navy.

There are still watermen working the Thames. Every boat carrying passengers from the various London piers to places like Hampton Court, Kew, Greenwich and the Thames Barrier, or hired as a pleasure boat by companies or individuals, is captained and crewed by watermen.

Bedlam

Throughout history there have been hospitals where the mentally ill are cared for. In 2830BC Egypt's Temple of Imhotep became a medical school that used gentle therapies to treat its patients, but over the centuries the attitude to these unfortunate people became more hostile, and 'mad-doctors' were convinced they were at best raving beasts who felt neither pain, nor heat, nor cold, and at worst sinners possessed by devils.

The most famous hospital is the Bethlem, or Bethlehem Royal Hospital in London, which was established as a priory in 1247 but came to be used solely as an asylum under Henry VIII. So terrible were the conditions in this place that Bedlam (short for Bethlem) became a byword for uproar and confusion. The inmates were chained to the walls or floor, whipped, kept naked on beds of straw and fed through the bars of their cages.

In the eighteenth century Bedlam became a popular tourist attraction. All classes of people, from the poorest to the aristocracy, paid to stroll through the asylum, laughing and jeering at the inmates and prodding them with long sticks to enrage them even further.

Today the Bethlehem Royal Hospital is sited in Beckenham, Kent, and mentally ill patients are treated with the care and respect they deserve.

The Met

Until Prime Minister Robert Peel created the Metropolitan Police Force in 1829 there were no law enforcers in London apart from parish watchmen and constables, known as Charlies, and the Bow Street Horse and Foot Patrol (the 'Bow Street Runners'), who pursued criminals detective-style on behalf of the magistrates.

These 'peelers', 'bobbies', 'crushers', 'cops' (because they 'copped' criminals) and 'bluebottles' (their uniforms were blue) were unpopular, since people perceived them as interfering.

Weighed down with a truncheon, a bull's eye lantern, a rattle (a heavier and louder version of the kind used at football matches today) and handcuffs, they 'plodded' the streets at a steady, dignified pace, taking care lest someone accidentally or deliberately try to empty the contents of a chamber pot on to their shiny top hats.

Their pay was poor and they worked twelve hours a day, three hundred and sixty-five days a year, although they were entitled to one week of unpaid holiday. They were obliged to wear their uncomfortable uniform at all times, even when off duty, and were not allowed to stop for a meal, so they ate while they walked their beat, and drank at public drinking fountains.

Gradually the new force grew in number and in popularity with the public as people began to realize that the police were there to help and not hinder them. At least, that was the thinking among law-abiding citizens. The criminal community begs to differ . . .

A Glossary of Victorian Slang and Phrases

Neither Jem, Ned, Billy nor the author made up any of the words or expressions in this book, even the golopshus ones. They were all part of common speech in Victorian times.

Area	Small space in front of the basement of a house
Ballast getter	A man whose job is to put heavy stones in the bilge of ships to keep them stable
Beak	Magistrate
Bear's grease	This was used to style and nourish hair; usually actually hog's or veal fat, scented and coloured
Bedlam	Hospital for mental illnesses, where conditions were appalling and the public could pay to view the inmates
Bigamy	The crime of marrying someone when already married
Black cap	Hat put on by a judge to pass a death sentence
Bosh	Nonsense
Bracelets	Handcuffs
Bread basket	Stomach
Buzzer	Pickpocket

Cesspit	A pit for the disposal of liquid waste and sewage
Chain locker	Compartment where the anchor chain is stored
Chapel of ease	Toilet (nickname)
Chimney-pot hat	Black silk cylindrical hat worn by gentlemen (nickname)
Chokey	Jail
Clack box	Chatterbox
Clink	Jail
Cop	Catch/punish
Copperplate	A style of neat handwriting, usually slanted and looped
Crusher	Policeman
Dobbin	Pet name for a large, gentle horse
Dogs are barking	Feet are hurting
Done up	Worn outdone in
Drink	River
Firkydoodling	Flirting/kissing and cuddling
Fluff it	Take it away, I don't want it
Gammon	Deceive/trick/persuade
Gib-faced	Ugly
Golopshus	Delicious
Goosecap	Silly person
Greenhorn	Inexperienced person, easily caught or tricked
Greensward	Lawn
Grub	Food

Gull	*Deceive/trick*
Hell and Tommy!	*Utter destruction!*
Hook it	*Go away*
Hostelry	*An inn, with food, entertainment and lodging*
Hurdy-gurdy	*Barrel organ, an instrument on which music is played by turning a handle*
Hussy	*Insulting term for a girl or woman, who may be behaving in a shameful way*
I'll be jiggered	*I'm amazed!*
In a kick	*In a moment*
Kiss in the Ring	*Game where players stand in a ring with hands joined, except one who runs round outside the ring and touches (or drops a handkerchief behind) one of the opposite sex, who leaves the ring and runs after the first, kissing him or her if they catch them before the toucher completes the circle and fills the gap*
Knacker's yard	*Where worn-out or diseased horses are slaughtered*
Latrine	*Toilet*
Lighterman	*One who works on a lighter, a boat used for unloading or sometimes loading ships that cannot be unloaded directly at a wharf*
Lock-up	*Jail*
Lumper	*Labourer employed in loading and unloading cargoes, especially timber*

Lushy	Drunk
Magsman	Street swindler
Molly grubs	Stomach ache
Nark	Informer/spy, as in 'Pigs' nark' — one who spies for the police
Navvy	Construction worker
Oh crimes	Oh no
Pack off	Go away
Paff!	Nonsense
Perfidy	Deceitfulness/treachery
Plummy	Top quality
Poxy	Poor quality/useless/annoying
Quack medicines	Pretend medicines sold by an unqualified person
Queer in the attic	Crazy
Rumbumtious	Unruly, cheeky
Scorf	Eat
Screever	Pavement artist
Shanks's pony	Walking
Shindig	Noisy disturbance
Shut your pan	Shut up
Snuffed it	Died
Sociable	Open four-wheeled carriage with facing seats
Splendacious/ splendiferous	Magnificent
Squally	Shrill/whiny

Stays	Corset stiffened with whalebone
Stow it	Shut up
Strung up	Killed by hanging
Take a carrot	Shut up
Thread My Grandmother's Needle	Game where players sing a song and hold hands to follow the leader in and out of arches made by other players' hands
Tipstaff	Hollow stick, with a tip of metal, carried by policemen and other officials until 1887 and containing a document proving the bearer's rank
Tumble	Realize/detect
Upper storey	Brain
Varmint	Rascal
Wag	Cheeky boy or man who thinks he is clever and amusing
Waterman	Boatman hired to carry passengers on a river
Wherry	Light rowing-boat used chiefly on rivers to carry passengers and goods for a fee
Wherryman	Man employed on a wherry
Whim-wham	Nonsense
Wideawake	Hat with a wide brim and shallow crown

Also by Bowering Sivers

Jammy Dodgers on the Run

London has never been so splendiferous — or so scarifyin' . . .

Jem, Ned and Billy are the Jammy Dodgers, three scruffy urchns always up to their eyeballs in scams and swindles. But the troublemaking trio meet their match the night they stray into the sinister slums — and Billy gets nabbed. Can Jem and Ned cook up a plummy plan to rescue their brother? Or has little Billy gone for good?

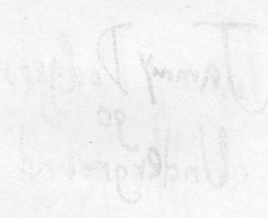

Jammy Dodgers go Underground

Jem, Ned and Billy are the Jammy Dodgers – three boys who pride themselves on being able to beg, borrow or blag their way out of a tight spot. The Perkinski brothers can slide out of trouble as smoothly as a jellied eel, and always land jammy side up.

Except for the fateful night when, down on their luck, the boys take a wrong turn. They wind up locked away in a workhouse. But the Jammy Dodgers aren't easily beaten, and where there's a will there's a way out . . . As escape routes go though, this one stinks.

Jammy Dodgers get Filthy Rich

London's high life can sometimes be downright dangerous . . .

Jem, Ned and Billy are the Jammy Dodgers – three boys who stick together through bad (and worse) on the dirty streets of London. But when a little Billy gets the chance to live in a posh house, it leaves his brothers out in the cold. Can Jem and Ned come up with their own plan to get rich quick?

TONY ROBINSON

The Worst Children's Jobs in History

The Worst Children's Jobs in History takes you back to the days when being a kid was no excuse for getting out of hard labour. This book tells the stories of the children throughout Britain's history whose work fed the nation, kept trains running and put clothes on everyone's backs.

Next time you find yourself having to listen to your parents, grandparents, uncles, neighbours and random old people in the supermarket telling you how much harder they had it in their day, ask them if they were a jigger-turner or a turnip-picker.
No? An orderly boy, perhaps? A stepper? Maybe they spent their weekends making matchboxes? Still no? Then they have no idea about the real meaning of hard work.